Stopping criminal activity wherever it happens. The agents at TCD are ready for anything.

More and more, federal law agencies have to mobilize to remote locations to address large-scale crime scenes and criminal activity—terror, hostage situations, kidnappings, shootings and the like. Because of the growing concerns and ever-increasing need for quick response times to these criminal events, the bureau created a specialized tech and tactical team combining experts from several active divisions—Weapons, Crime Scene Investigation, Protection, Negotiation, IT. Because they are a smaller unit, they are more nimble for rapid deployment and assistance to address various situations. This joint team of agents is known as the Tactical Crime Division.

ROOKIE INSTINCTS

CAROL ERICSON

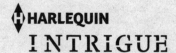

Special thanks and acknowledgment are given to
Carol Ericson for her contribution to the
Tactical Crime Division: Traverse City miniseries.

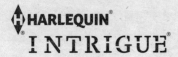

HARLEQUIN®
INTRIGUE®

ISBN-13: 978-1-335-13681-7

Rookie Instincts

For questions and comments about the quality of this book,
please contact us at CustomerService@Harlequin.com.

Harlequin Enterprises ULC
22 Adelaide St. West, 40th Floor
Toronto, Ontario M5H 4E3, Canada
www.Harlequin.com

Printed in U.S.A.

Carol Ericson is a bestselling, award-winning author of more than forty books. She has an eerie fascination for true-crime stories, a love of film noir and a weakness for reality TV, all of which fuel her imagination to create her own tales of murder, mayhem and mystery. To find out more about Carol and her current projects, please visit her website at www.carolericson.com, "where romance flirts with danger."

Books by Carol Ericson

Visit the Author Profile page at Harlequin.com.

CAST OF CHARACTERS

Aria Calletti—A new member of the FBI's Tactical Crime Division and a narcotics specialist. Her first case is right up her alley, but Aria's resolve to shine as a professional among her new team members hits a roadblock in the solid—and sexy—form of the brother of one of the victims.

Grayson Rhodes—Working undercover on the docks of Port Huron to find his missing sister and her baby, this Detroit businessman has stumbled onto a drug-smuggling operation, and the only person he can trust is a green FBI agent who sends his protective instincts into overdrive.

Chloe Larsen—A young mother with a drug problem, she gets into business with the wrong people and pays with her life.

Tony Balducci—A dockworker with dreams of the highlife, he's an easy pawn for a drug-smuggling ring...and the FBI's only hope of cracking it.

Brandy—This young woman discovers she's made a deal with the devil, but will her realization come too late to save her?

Alana Suzuki—The director of the FBI's Tactical Crime Division is a professional at the top of her game, but some cases affect her more than others, and this one hits her where it hurts most.

Prologue

The wind whipped off the lake, its chilly tentacles snaking into his thin black jacket, which he gathered at the neck with one raw hand, stiff with the cold. His other hand dipped into his pocket, his fingers curling around the handle of the gun.

His eyes darted toward the dark, glassy water and the rowboat bobbing against the shore before he stepped onto the road…and behind his prey.

She hobbled ahead of him, her shoes crunching the gravel, her body tilted to one side as she gripped her heavy cargo, which swung back and forth, occasionally banging against her leg.

A baby. *Nobody said nothing about a baby.*

He took a few steps after her and the sound of his boots grinding into the gravel seemed to echo through the still night. He froze.

When her footsteps faltered, he veered back into the reeds and sand bordering the lake. He couldn't have her spotting him and running off. What would she do with the baby? She couldn't run carrying a car seat. He'd hauled one of those things before with his niece inside and it wasn't no picnic, even though Mindy was just a little thing.

He crept on silent feet, covering three or four steps to her one until he was almost parallel with her. Close enough to hear her singing some Christmas lullaby. Close enough to hear that baby gurgle a response.

The chill in the air stung his nose and he wiped the back of his hand across it. He licked his chapped lips.

Nobody said nothing about a baby.

The girl stopped, her pretty voice dying out, the car seat swinging next to her, the toys hooked onto the handle swaying and clacking. She turned on the toes of her low-heeled boots and peered at the road behind her, the whites of her eyes visible in the dark.

But he wasn't on the road no more.

He stepped onto the gravel from the brush that had been concealing him. Her head jerked in his direction. Her mouth formed a surprised *O*, but her eyes knew.

When he leveled his weapon at her, she didn't even try to run. Her knees dipped as she placed the car seat on the ground next to her feet.

She huffed out a sigh that carried two words. "My baby."

He growled. "I ain't gonna hurt the baby."

Then he shot her through the chest.

The sound of the shot buffeted his eardrums, and a few birds screeched and took flight, but there was nobody here to help her or her baby…just him.

The girl had crumpled to the ground, her knees drawn up, her hand flung out to the side, inches from the car seat. If her lullaby had put the baby to sleep, the gunshot had awakened him and he wailed as if he knew his momma was gone.

He shuffled forward and hovered over the body. Brushing aside the brown hair that had swept across her neck, he placed a finger at her throat. Her pulse had stopped. Her song had ended.

With the sound of the gunshot dead in the night, the baby's howls faded into squishy, blubbery sobs.

"Shh. Don't cry, little buddy." All babies looked the same to him, but this one had a blue beanie on his head and a blue blanket dotted with panda bears tucked around his body. His sister always dressed her daughter in pink just so everyone would know she was a girl.

The baby hiccupped and put a knuckle in his mouth, his blue watery eyes wide.

"That's it, little buddy. I ain't gonna leave you out here for long." He retrieved a crumpled tissue from the front pocket of his jeans and dabbed the baby's damp cheeks and runny nose. He didn't bother to blot the blood spots on the blanket.

Then he shoved his hand into his cheap jacket and withdrew a plastic bag, whispery smooth between his fingers. He wiped off his fingerprints with the edge of his shirt and, still pinching the bag with fingers poked into his shirt, leaned over the dead girl and tucked the bag of Dance Fever in her purse. The bullet hadn't touched the strap. It remained crossed over her body, soaked with the blood still oozing from her chest.

"Just a few more minutes, little buddy." He dipped into his pocket once more and pulled out the burner phone they'd given him. They should've said something about the baby at the same time.

He flipped up the phone and called 9-1-1. When the operator answered, he pitched his voice low and scratchy. "Yeah, there's a baby in a car seat down by the lake all by himself. Looks abandoned."

"Where are you sir? Is the baby hurt?"

He gave the operator directions to the gravel road snaking beside the lake, flipped the phone shut and walked back to his boat, whistling the lullaby.

Chapter One

Humming off-key, Aria punched the elevator button with her knuckle and then wiped her clammy palms on the thighs of her black slacks. When the doors whispered open, she stepped inside the car and released a breath as she stared at her mottled reflection on the elevator doors.

She slid her finger beneath the elastic band that held her hair back and pulled it out. She shook her head to loosen the strands over her shoulders. The ponytail begged, *Take me seriously.* She didn't need props to get that message across to her coworkers.

She shrugged out of her black wool coat, leaving the purple scarf twined around her neck. Squaring her shoulders, she said aloud, "Oh, the scarf? Too busy to notice I still had it on."

She snorted and unwound the scarf, leaving two purple-fringed ends hanging to her waist. The elevator dinged and she stood at attention until the doors opened on the seventh floor.

Hiking her laptop case on her shoulder, she strode down the hallway to the conference room, the heels of her black boots clicking on the floor in a steady, confident beat.

The door to the conference room yawned open on a large space with a gleaming, oval table in the center and two large video screens on either side of the room. A smaller desk hunched in the corner, overflowing with a laptop, an abundance of cords and a variety of AV equipment. The only other person in the room, a curvaceous bottled-blonde with a colorful clip in her hair, hovered over the computer. With a flash of red lipstick, she gave Aria a quick smile and a wink and returned to her work.

Director Alana Suzuki, smart in a navy pantsuit with a snowy-white blouse, barreled through the door. "You made it." She thrust out her hand to Aria, her eyes gleaming behind translucent-framed glasses. "Welcome aboard. I'll do the introductions when everyone gets here. Take any seat around the table."

"Director Suzuki." Aria gripped the older woman's hand, giving as good as she got. "Glad to be here."

"Alana, please." She ran a hand through her short black hair, unapologetically peppered with gray. "We're an informal bunch here."

The woman tapping away at the computer called out. "Uh, you might want to revise the invitation to take any seat. There's no assigned seating, but everyone always claims the same spot. Habit or security."

Alana waved her hand at the other woman. "Don't pay any attention to Opaline. She's our tech guru and her mind works in mysterious ways. Opaline, this is our new team member, Aria Calletti. Aria, Opaline Lopez."

Opaline raised her hand and wiggled her fingers, her long nails matching the red of her lips.

Aria cleared her throat. "Nice to meet you."

With Opaline's words about the seating hanging in the air, Aria folded her arms across her bag and wedged a shoulder against the wall. She didn't want to ruffle anyone's feathers on her first day.

As long as you played by the rules, went by the book, you'd fit in. She'd discovered that as a beat cop on the mean streets of Detroit. Go along, get along and do your job.

The other team members started to filter into the room, a few in pairs, a few on their own. As Aria glanced at each person, his or her name flashed into her brain. She'd done her research on the Tactical Crime Division team when Director Suzuki—Alana—had invited her to apply for it. And apply she did.

She'd given up her job with the Detroit PD and hit the ground running at the FBI Academy in Quantico. Five months later, she'd taken the assignment with the TCD and was ready to hit the ground running again.

A few of the team members nodded at her as they grabbed seats. Aria had pretended to be looking through her bag to explain her delay in taking her place at the table—with the big boys and girls. When everyone seemed settled in, she slid into a seat next to Supervisory Special Agent Axel Morrow, his large frame dwarfing the chair.

His blue eyes assessed her as she scooted her chair forward, making her glad she'd opted for slacks and a jacket but regretting the loss of her ponytail.

Alana stood at one end of the table and commanded the room. At just over five feet tall, her physical stature was not responsible for the snap to attention, all eyes on her, conversations dying out. The woman had a presence—an erect, military bearing that radiated confidence and demanded respect.

She had Aria folding her hands on the table in front of her like a schoolgirl.

"Welcome back, everyone. I want to congratulate you on the successful completion of Operation Lollipop. A job well done."

The room erupted in applause and Aria joined in. She'd read the files on the human trafficking case and couldn't wait to be part of this team that did so much good.

"Okay, okay." Alana held up her hand. "Don't get too carried away. We have the next case on our plate. Before I get into that…we have a new team member I'd like to introduce Aria Calletti. She can say a few words about herself and then we can go around the room and you can tell her who you are. Try to keep it under a minute, Opaline."

The other team members chuckled, as Opaline tapped a finger to her chest, her heavily mascaraed eyes wide.

As she took her seat, Alana nodded in Aria's direction. "Tell us a little something about yourself, Aria."

Aria cleared her throat. "I grew up in Holland, Michigan, and joined the PD in Detroit. Due to my age, I did a lot of undercover work in narcotics, especially at the schools, and worked dope as a beat cop. While working as a cop, I put myself through Wayne State, criminal justice major. Got lucky on a big case and helped bring down a drug kingpin. That's when Director Suzuki invited me to apply to the FBI with this division as my goal."

Axel, Alana's second-in-command, held up a finger. "That's 'Alana' to you. We're not into formalities."

Selena Lopez, the K-9 handler, her dark hair in a sleek chignon, nudged Axel in the shoulder. "And don't you dare call Axel 'Supervisory Special Agent Morrow.' He hates that."

"She's right. We're on a first-name basis around here." Axel rubbed his arm. "Impressive stuff, Aria."

Alana took off her glasses and hunched over the table. "Yeah, that was a little more than luck, Aria. Her investigative work was instrumental in bringing down that dirtbag. That's why she's a perfect fit for this team. Anything else you want to tell us?"

Anything else…such as how she felt as if her entire career hinged on her ability to pull her own weight on this team? Such as how she felt like an imposter? That her real self was that distorted image in the elevator door?

"That's it." Aria pressed her lips together and eked out a small smile.

"You, go." Alana leveled a finger at Opaline in the corner.

"We met earlier because I was the first person here, as usual." Opaline wiggled her fingers in the air. "I'm the tech support for this motley crew. They'd fail miserably without me. Oh, and I heard you had a bunch of brothers who are firefighters, so if any of them are single I'm willing and able…and that was well under a minute."

Aria shot a quick glance at the K-9 handler, Selena Lopez. She'd read in the bios that these two were sisters. Selena's tight smile and clenched hands in front of her told Aria nothing…well, almost nothing.

"I'll go next." The tall, cool blonde sitting across from Aria held her up hand. "I'm Carly Welsh. I've been on TCD for three years, and before that, I was with the FBI in Detroit. So, we have that in common, Aria. Welcome to the squad."

Selena spoke up, her low voice vibrating. "That's *Dr.* Carly Welsh. She's got a Ph.D. in biological warfare."

Aria's gaze darted back to Carly, a rosy hue washing over the blonde's pale cheeks. The knots in Aria's gut twisted a little more.

The brooding man at the end of the table ran a hand over the top of his head. "I guess I'll go next. I'm Max McRay. Explosives. Did a stint in the Army. Looking forward to working with you, Aria."

Axel put a hand over his mouth and coughed. "War hero."

Aria nodded at Max. He hadn't mentioned the fact that he'd lost the lower half of his left leg to a bomb in Afghanistan. Although he'd had a slight hitch in his step when he'd walked into the conference room, if Aria hadn't read his bio, she wouldn't have known about his leg.

"I'm Selena Lopez." Selena put her long, slender fingers in the air and wiggled them, just as Opaline had done. "My *raison d'être* on this team is surveillance and tracking. My partner's a white shepherd named Blanca, and if she doesn't like you... I don't know, Aria."

"Blanca's a good judge of character." Axel tugged on the lapels of his jacket. "She happens to love me."

Max shot back. "That's because you give her treats when Selena's back is turned."

"Busted." Carly flicked a rolled-up piece of paper at Axel, who caught it easily in one hand.

Aria's lips stretched into a smile. The relaxed camaraderie of the team tightened those knots in her belly even more. Would she ever be able to engage in this friendly back-and-forth?

She'd never been one of the boys on the PD; had always felt like she had her nose pressed against the glass. As the only girl in a family of five siblings, she was accustomed to that feeling. Her brothers loved her, of course, but were overly protective and, like Rudolph, she'd never joined in their reindeer games.

Axel bobbled the ball of paper Carly had fired at him between his palms, his blue eyes alight. "I'm Supervisory Special Agent Axel Morrow. You can call me Axel or Axe. I would say that I'm Alana's right hand, but we all know that honor belongs to Amanda over there, furiously taking notes on her laptop."

The cute redhead seated next to Alana peered over the top of her computer and grinned. "You got that right."

Aria studied Axel as he reeled off his background—his work background. His gift of gab must be one of the reasons for his top skills as a hostage negotiator. He could probably get anyone to do anything. At the FBI Academy, they'd studied some of Axel's criminal profiles for their insight and accuracy.

Now, Aria narrowed her eyes at the good-looking blond and practiced a little profiling of her own. Did he use his charming manner to mask the tragedy of his young life?

"That's me in a nutshell, but feel free to ask any of us anything anytime. We're here to help you." He flattened a hand over his heart. "Great to have you on board, Aria."

"Now, for my true right hand, last but certainly not least, Amanda Orton." Alana tapped the redhead on the shoulder.

Amanda stopped typing. "I'm Amanda Orton. I'm Alana's assistant. If you want to reach Alana or schedule a meeting with her, you come through me."

"And if you want to get to Amanda, you have to go through that massive security guard downstairs, who happens to be her husband." Axel raised his eyebrows. "You see him? He looks like a linebacker for the Lions."

"You do not need to go through him to see me." Amanda's lips and eyes turned up at the corners. "You can reach me anytime, Aria, and I'm the keeper of the birthday club so I need to get that from you at some point."

Carly rolled her eyes. "As if we need to be reminded of our birthdays every year."

"Let me know when you want it, and I'll give it to you." Aria tucked her hair behind one ear. "Thanks for introducing yourselves. I'm so impressed with your work, and I can't wait to be a contributing member of this team."

Silence. Ugh, had she laid it on too thick?

"The only one missing is Rihanna Clark. She's our PR person. She interacts with the media, the local PDs and crime victims. She had a meeting today," Alana said, rapping on the table and pushing to her feet. "Now that the niceties are out of the way, we have work to do. Opaline?"

Opaline clicked her keyboard and the oversize TV screens on either side of the room came to life—only to show death. Two young women, both on their backs, sprawled on the ground, a gaping gunshot wound in their chests.

Alana aimed a pointer at the split-screen, the red laser hovering over the bodies. "Two victims in Port Huron. Both near the lake, different roads. Single gunshot to the chest, point-blank. The Port Huron police don't have any leads yet but…"

The next slide jumped onto to the screen and Amanda gasped. "I-is that a baby?"

"It is." Alana clenched her jaw. "A baby in a car seat was next to the most recent victim. Child Protective Services has the baby now, and the PD ordered DNA tests to determine if the baby belongs with the dead woman."

Max growled. "Was the baby hurt?"

"The baby is fine, which is how the second body was discovered. Someone called in an abandoned baby.

Didn't mention the dead body next to the baby, but reported the baby."

"Was it the killer?" Axel hunched forward, the veins popping out of his forearms, hands clenched.

Alana shook her head. "We don't know. He didn't leave a name or contact info, but could just be a scared bystander."

Selena asked, "Did they trace the call?"

"Cell phone. No info on that phone yet."

Opaline looked up, shoving her glasses higher on her nose. "I'm looking into the phone now."

"Has the PD identified the victims? Do they have any similarities?" Carly scribbled on a notepad in front of her.

"The first victim had opioids in her system, too soon for toxicology on the second victim, and both had a small amount of fentanyl on them—packaged to sell."

Alana tipped her head at Aria, and Aria squared her shoulders. Fentanyl she knew, along with all its street names: China Girl, Dance Fever, Apache, Goodfella, and on and on.

Alana continued. "Both women were about the same age, brown hair, brown eyes, not sex workers—at least, not known to the PD—and they were dressed conservatively. They did both have ID on them."

Selena slumped in her seat. "That makes things a little easier."

"Not quite." Alana took a big breath. "The IDs they had were identical."

Aria blurted out, "Identical?"

"That's right. These women not only look alike, they

were carrying IDs that have the same name, same address, same height, same weight. For all intents and purposes? The same girl died twice."

Chapter Two

Aria hunched her shoulders as a chill shot up her spine. "Someone's going through a lot of trouble to give these women the same ID only to kill them."

Max scratched his jaw. "Maybe their deaths are part of a plan nobody told them about, but what kind of plan calls for two identical women?"

"I'm assuming the PD already checked that person and address?" Selena's short nails clicked on the mahogany surface of the table as she drummed her fingers. "Is she a real person?"

"The name on the ID is Maddie Johnson. Fake. Everything fake down to the Port Huron address, which doesn't exist." Alana pressed a button on the remote in her hand and gestured toward the screen now displaying two fraudulent IDs side by side. They were identical except for the pictures of the dead women.

"If that was the killer on the phone—" Axel pushed back from the table and crossed his ankle over his knee "—why'd he make the call? Why'd he spare the baby?"

"Thank God, he did," Max replied. "So, we're not dealing with a total monster."

"Maybe he likes puppies, too." Carly's brown eyes darkened to two chips of coal. "The guy murdered two women…a woman with a baby."

Max held up his hands. "I'm not saying he should win the Nobel Peace Prize, but leaving the baby untouched tells us something about him. Something we can use."

Aria had pulled out her laptop during the discussion and had been taking her own notes, although she figured they'd all get a copy of Amanda's. Without looking up from her keyboard, she asked, "Do we know the grade of fentanyl they were carrying?"

Dead air hung over the room and Aria glanced up to find several pairs of eyes on her.

Max broke the silence. "Is that important? Should we know that?"

Her gaze traveled across the different expressions— curious, piqued, encouraging—and she said, "Yes. Sometimes we can trace the packaging and the purity to a specific dealer."

"Didn't know that." Selena formed her fingers into a gun and pointed at Aria. "That would definitely help. Good call, Aria."

Aria held up one finger. "Another thing about the location of the bodies and the drugs… Port Huron is a border town on the water. It's a prime location for smuggling. The packets of Dance Fever those women had could be part of a larger ring moving drugs across the border."

As Alana clicked through the rest of the slides and the team bandied about more ideas, the tension that had been gripping Aria's shoulders, tension she hadn't even realized she had, began slipping away. She could do this.

An hour later, Alana put up the last slide—the baby in the car seat, a set of oversize plastic keys in primary colors and a little fuzzy sheep clipped to the handle. "Good start, people. Remember why we're doing this. This little guy lost his mother. Someone lost a daughter, a sister, maybe a wife. Go home, get your affairs in order and we'll meet at the airport. Private plane will take us to Port Huron at four o'clock sharp."

Opaline ended the slide show, Amanda put the finishing touches on the meeting notes, and the team members began gathering their laptops, notepads, pens and coffee cups.

Axel's voice rose above the rest. "Good hire, boss. Aria has a lot to offer."

Max reached across the table, extending his hand. "I'm excited about what you can bring to the team, Aria."

She smiled and nodded, giddiness bubbling in her veins.

They all seemed confident she could do the job. Now she just had to convince herself.

As the sun set, the TCD's private plane touched down in Mount Clemens. Port Huron didn't have an airport, so the Selfridge Air National Guard allowed them to fly onto the base, which was about forty-five minutes from Port Huron.

The descent provided Aria with a bird's-eye view of

the area, near two lakes and not far from the Canadian border. The proximity to water and the border confirmed her suspicions about drug smuggling. But why kill the smugglers? Why kill the young women willing to do your bidding?

Dealers exacted rough justice on the street sellers, the runners and the smugglers whenever they started bucking the system or tried to circumvent it. If a smuggler decided to go into business by herself, started using the product instead of shipping it, or got cold feet, or worse, turned informant, she would most likely end up meeting the business end of a gun.

Carly leaned across the aisle of the plane, her blond hair spilling like sunshine over her shoulder. "At least we get our own rooms at the hotel this time. Sometimes we have to share. That means Selena and I usually bunk together, the guys pair up, and Amanda and Rihanna share. Alana always has her own room. She claims it's because she snores."

"Opaline doesn't come along?" Aria cranked her head over her shoulder. She'd noticed the tech specialist's absence when she'd boarded.

"Usually she stays in Traverse City, and sometimes Rihanna goes where she's needed. Rihanna's already in Port Huron. She came out here yesterday to take charge of the baby and make sure he's placed with a foster family while the police ID his mom." Carly blinked her golden lashes rapidly. "Poor little thing."

Pressing a hand to her heart, Aria said, "I just keep thinking how terrified his mom must've been when the killer pointed that gun at her. Her last thoughts must've been for the safety of her baby."

Carly stretched one long denim-clad leg into the aisle, the heel of her suede boot digging into the thin carpet. "She probably thought her killer was going to shoot her baby, too. I can't even imagine."

"Why didn't he?" The plane finished taxiing, its wheels squealing to a stop, the engines cutting out. "Why'd a cold-blooded killer spare a baby?"

"Maybe he knew the victim. Port Huron isn't exactly a big city, is it? Perhaps he didn't know the identity of his target until he faced her."

"So, you're saying someone ordered a hit." Aria reached down and pulled her purse from beneath the seat in front of her.

"Based on the duplicate IDs and the drugs, it has to be. Wouldn't it?" Raising her eyebrows, Carly tilted her head.

"Unless the killer is a fellow smuggler and got jealous or made it personal." Aria released her seat belt. "Just trying to look at all angles here."

"No, that's good. Keep it coming, Aria. That's what makes this team so great—everyone coming from different places, everyone contributing their own ideas. Your theory also gives another reason why that killer had a soft spot for the baby." Carly stood and pulled her designer luggage from the overhead compartment, setting it in front of her.

Aria blew out a breath. The theory had made sense to her, but she was glad it made sense to Dr. Welsh, too.

Aria shuffled off the plane with the rest of the team

and headed down the steps to the tarmac where a black van awaited them. After the driver loaded their luggage and equipment, Blanca, Selena's K-9, jumped in the back.

The brisk air carried the scent of fish and brine, and Aria's fingertips buzzed with impatience. She'd have to sit through a dinner tonight and actually try to get some sleep, but the investigation started tomorrow.

They were still awaiting ballistics from this most recent murder, to see if it matched the first victim, and on toxicology reports for the second victim and the baby. The DNA would take longer.

They piled into the van and Aria scooted into the very back, next to the window.

Alana took the seat next to Aria and patted her knee. "We'll spare the tall people the trouble of crawling back here, but I'm not going to be very good company. The ride to Port Huron is long enough for me to pull out my laptop and get in a little work."

"Go ahead." Aria dropped her voice. "We shouldn't be discussing the case in front of the driver, anyway, right?"

"No, but I'm not all business all the time. I'd like to get to know you better on a personal level, Aria. I make a point to learn as much about my agents as I can." Alana winked. "Figure out what makes them all tick."

From the seat in front of them, Carly twisted her head around. "Watch out for Alana. She has a knack for getting to our deepest, darkest secrets. She should be the one interrogating all our suspects. She'd give Axe a run for his money."

Alana pulled her computer out of her bag and positioned it on her lap. "The better I get to know you, the more smoothly the team runs."

The van stopped at the gate on the way off the base and then hit the highway north to Port Huron. Max sat in the front seat and chatted with the driver, who was retired Army. Axel and Selena sat behind them, their heads together, exchanging whispers, probably work-related, and Carly and Amanda had claimed the middle row, each glued to her phone.

As Alana tapped away on her keyboard, Aria stuffed some earbuds in her ears and listened to classical music. She leaned her head against the cool glass and watched the scenery pass by. She couldn't see much in the darkness, but occasionally a freeway sign would pop up with the miles remaining to Canada, reminding her just how close they were to the border.

Almost forty minutes later, the van took the turnoff toward downtown Port Huron. As they rolled past the lake, Aria cupped her hand over the glass and gazed at the gleaming water, boats bobbing in the docks, a few decked out with colorful Christmas lights that reflected off the lake's dark surface.

Aria squinted so that the lights blurred in a rainbow pattern. Somewhere out there, another brown-haired, brown-eyed young woman with dreams of financial security in her eyes and packets of Dance Fever in her pocket, faced potential danger.

And unsuspecting families sat on a precipice of the most devastating news of their lives.

THE WIND GUSTED and the halyards on the docked boats clanged against the masts, chiming out quittin' time. Grayson grabbed the rope attached to the last pallet he'd loaded for the day. The rough hemp dug into his palms, already toughened from a few days' work on the docks.

He dragged the pallet to the warehouse and hoisted it on top of a stack, ready for tomorrow morning.

Chuck smacked him on the back, the contact from the former hockey player and now his coworker reverberating in his chest. "Good work today, Gary. Some of the boys are going for a beer. Wanna come along?"

"Thanks, Chuck. Maybe next time." Grayson rolled down the sleeves of his denim work shirt, the cold air finally soaking into his skin now that the heavy lifting had come to a backbreaking end. "I'm still dealing with stuff from my landlord in the new place. He's supposed to fix the toilet tonight."

"Yeah, you gotta watch these landlords. They'll try to skip out on paying for anything." Chuck spit on the ground. "Rich bastards."

"I got my eye on this guy, and I plan to hold his feet to the fire." Grayson thrust out his fist for a bump. "Hit me up next time for a brewski."

Chuck plowed his raw, reddened knuckles into Grayson's. "You got it, man. We'll hoist one for you tonight."

Grayson held up his hand to a few of the other guys as he headed for the used truck he'd bought yesterday. He climbed in and gripped the steering wheel, his own knuckles abraded, staring at the docks over the rim.

Despite his reason for being on the docks in Port Huron, the work invigorated him. The soreness of his muscles when he ran a marathon or worked out at the gym didn't equate to the ache that permeated his bones after a few days loading and unloading cargo. This pain felt righteous.

He snorted. He'd better not utter that sentiment to the men, and the woman, he worked with on the dock. They'd kick his ass for that...rich bastard.

He cranked on the engine and blasted the heat. Reaching under the front seat, he retrieved his cell phone. He didn't carry it on the job. Didn't want anyone getting a look at his texts or photos.

With a knot in his gut, he checked his calls and texts. After thumbing through a few work-related issues and listening to his assistant, Patrick, whine in not one but two voice mails, he slumped in his seat.

Nothing from the police yet. Not that he expected anything. The guy at the front desk of the Port Huron PD could barely keep his eyes open when Grayson had gone in to file the missing persons report. There'd been one unidentified dead woman, but she hadn't matched the description Grayson had given the officer...in more ways than one.

He slammed his hands against the steering wheel. Where the hell was she? If the police didn't give a damn, he'd have to do his own searching.

He hadn't heard anything on the docks yet, but he hadn't been there that long. He still had hope of gleaning some information from the guys as they started to loosen up more, accept him as one of their own. That beer tonight would've gone a long way toward that end, but he had his own mission after work—and it didn't include a broken toilet.

By the time he pulled out of the parking lot, the other workers' vehicles had disappeared. Who wanted to hang around the commercial end of the dock once you punched your time card?

Grayson eyed the lake as it curved around to the noncommercial side of the dock where pleasure boats, fishing boats and a few small rowboats clustered, some already decorated with Christmas lights. Already? Thanksgiving was last week with Christmas right around the corner. The realization punched him in the gut. Thanksgiving should've been a joyous holiday, a prelude to Christmas.

He cruised along the street that bordered the shoreline and turned into the parking lot for the noncommercial harbor. Boats, all this water—it would be easy for someone to disappear.

He clambered out of the truck and trudged down to the wooden dock, the cold air biting at his cheeks. Shoving his hands into his pockets, he stooped his shoulders and gazed at the nodding boats, talking to each other in creaks and sighs.

Lights emanated from inside a couple of the larger sailboats. He knew that a few hardy souls lived on their boats full-time, but he'd already identified and dismissed them as possible sources of information.

His head jerked sideways as the sound of clicking heels came from the other side of one of the bigger boats. He squinted into the distance and his heart skipped a beat when he saw a young woman in a dark coat, dark jeans and what had to be boots, not deck shoes, to make that noise.

He took a step in her direction, a name on his lips, which he choked back when he saw the girl flip her dark hair over one shoulder. As she drew closer, passing beneath the glow from a light, Grayson released a long breath.

When she spotted him, her steps faltered, but she grabbed the strap of her purse and soldiered on toward the gate. She pushed through without giving him a second look.

She could be someone else's sister. "Hey, you should be careful walking around on your own out here at night."

Without turning her head, she gave him a one-fingered salute and yelled, "Mind your own damn business."

So much for being a good Samaritan. He twisted his head to the side and watched her cross the parking lot and walk up to the street, her stride purposeful, her shoulders back and the knit cap on her head bobbing up and down. At least she didn't look like a victim.

He watched the boats and the water for another fifteen minutes, not knowing what to expect. But instinct buzzing in his ear that this area held a clue to Chloe's disappearance, kept him rooted to the same spot.

The tip of his nose numb and his eyes stinging, he pushed away from the post he'd been clinging to with stiff fingers and returned to his truck.

If he hurried, he might catch the guys for a beer, but right now he couldn't carry off the jovial dockworker whose only care in the world was the Lions' dismal record.

Right now, all he cared about was finding his sister... and her seven-month-old baby.

Chapter Three

Rihanna Clark chucked the baby under the chin and jiggled the set of plastic keys in front of his face. "Hello, there, Baby Doe. You sure are cute."

The baby reached out with his chubby fist and curled his fingers, wet with drool, around the yellow key. He shoved the end into his mouth and gnawed on it with his gums.

Rihanna leaned forward and tapped Shereen North, the CPS social worker on the shoulder. "Is that okay? He has that key in his mouth."

Shereen looked in her rearview mirror and smiled. "That's fine. He's teething. I'm guessing his age is around six or seven months. He might be older if he has drugs in his system and some delayed development, but he looks healthy. You don't have children?"

Rihanna shrugged her shoulders and shook her head. After being attacked and held captive by a homicidal maniac a few years ago, she couldn't fathom the idea of bringing any children into this world.

Alana had assured her that she'd get over those fears one day, but she'd actually have to find a man she could trust. For now, she preferred admiring from afar and going goo-goo-gaga over someone else's baby.

"I hope he doesn't have drugs in his system." She reached over to the baby next to her in the back seat and stroked his cheek with her knuckle. "He seems too calm to have NAS."

"At seven months, he might be too old to display many of the characteristics of neonatal abstinence syndrome, but he'll be tested. If he's positive, we can work with that."

"If we don't find next of kin soon, is this foster family prepared to deal with that?"

"Rick and Sarah are among our best, and they have experience dealing with NAS babies. Rick works as a firefighter—in fact, that's how they started as foster parents. Rich was called out to a terrible fire that killed the parents of a baby. He and Sarah cared for that baby for a short time, and they were hooked. Sarah's a retired teacher. They have two grown sons, no grandchildren yet, and love these babies."

"They sound perfect. Let's just hope this is another short-term assignment." Rihanna pinched Baby Doe's toes through his soft suede moccasins. "This little guy needs his family...if they want him."

Ten minutes later, Shereen turned down a street of neatly groomed homes, smug in their middle-class comfort. She pulled in next to a red truck in the driveway of a home that had an actual white-picket fence.

Baby Doe dropped the key and the keychain slid down the handle of the car seat.

"Don't worry, baby boy. You're going to be in good

hands." She smoothed a finger over his silky blond hair, and he rewarded her with a look from his blue eyes. Given Mom's looks with the brown hair and brown eyes, Dad must be blond-haired and blue-eyed.

Shereen cut the engine and they both got out of the car. Rihanna lifted the latch of the gate to the walkway as Shereen circled around to get the baby.

Hearing their approach, Rick and Sarah emerged from the house and stood on the porch. Rick's arm curled around Sarah's shoulder, while Sarah clasped her hands in front of her, a smile lighting up her face. She had to have been a kindergarten teacher.

Rihanna's boots clipped on the pavers as she walked up to the porch. "Mr. and Mrs. Colby? I'm Rihanna Clark, the FBI's liaison on the murder case of the baby's mother—or, at least, we think she's his mother."

Sarah reached out and clasped Rihanna's hand, tugging her in for a hug that smelled like warm apples and cinnamon. "Thank you for bringing him to us. We'll cherish him as one of our own, until his people can be found and notified."

Rihanna inhaled the woman's homey scent and blinked back tears. Maybe Rick and Sarah could adopt her, too?

Just when Sarah released her, leaving her out in the cold, Rick dove in for a bear hug that almost swept Rihanna from her feet. He kept hold of Rihanna's hand and said, "I hope you Feds catch the SOB who did this to his mother."

"Rick, shh." Sarah patted his muscular arm. "Not in front of the baby."

Shereen had followed her to the porch, Baby Doe's car seat swinging from her hand, the keyring and fuzzy sheep dancing in the air.

Rick squeezed between the two women and lunged toward Shereen. "That looks heavy, Shereen. Let me take him."

Rick brought the baby into the house and set the car seat on the floor. Crouching, he released the straps, scooped Baby Doe out of the seat, and tucked him in the crook of his arm. "He's a big boy. Six months old? What do you think, Sarah?"

"I think he's a little angel."

As the two foster parents cooed over their new charge, Rihanna glanced around the room, her gaze lighting on a playpen outfitted with colorful toys, a battery-operated swing, a mat on the floor with an arched mobile and a spinning, rocking baby walker—a cornucopia of fun times for baby.

Although Rihanna knew all too well looks could be deceiving, CPS had solid, favorable reports of this couple, and Baby Doe couldn't be in better hands.

Rihanna cleared her throat. "We'll keep you posted on any information we have about the baby's identity and his family, including whether or not they'll be making a move for custody."

"Thank you, Rihanna." Sarah rested her cheek against the baby's head. "I'm sure Shereen told you, we're old hands at this. The baby is ours until he isn't."

Shereen withdrew a folder from the bag hanging over her shoulder. "You know the drill. I have some forms for you to sign before we leave."

"Kitchen table." Sarah turned to Rihanna with the baby in her arms. "Do you want to hold him for a few minutes while we take care of this, Rihanna?"

"Of course." Rihanna stepped forward, holding out her arms, and Baby Doe went willingly to her. This personable little guy must be accustomed to strangers. He hadn't let out one peep, except for happy babbles, ever since she and Shereen had picked him up from the hospital—the same hospital where his mother lay on a cold slab in the morgue.

Rihanna cuddled him close and then dipped her head, putting her lips next to the downy curve of his ear. "Don't worry, baby. Like Rick said, we're going to catch the SOB who took your momma away from you."

THE DINNER THE night before had been just what Aria needed. The rest of the special agents on the team had seemed almost human as they'd consumed actual food and drink instead of manna from heaven.

She'd gotten to know them a little better as individuals, especially Max, who'd been seated next to her. He'd lifted up his pant leg and showed her his artificial limb, explaining how the high-tech prosthesis worked. He also talked about his toddler son, which explained why he'd been one of the first agents in the meeting to show concern about the baby left with his dead mother, presumably.

The DNA on mother and child hadn't come back yet. They hadn't even received the autopsy report on the second victim, although cause of death was obvious—gunshot to the chest.

As Aria eyed the scoop of congealed oatmeal she'd plopped in her bowl from the hotel's complimentary breakfast bar, wondering if she'd made a mistake, Axel poked at her bowl with a spoon. "That looks disgusting."

"That doesn't look much better." With her fork, she tapped his plate, heaped with clumpy, orangey-yellow scrambled eggs and greasy sausage links.

"Breakfast of champions. And, speaking of disgusting—" he jerked his thumb over his shoulder at Carly, decked out in lululemon tights and a sleek running jacket, her blond hair scooped into a high ponytail "—get a load of her. She makes the rest of us look like slugs."

Aria flicked a glance at Axel's broad chest and biceps visible beneath his shirt. Not a very likely slug.

"How's the breakfast?" Carly grabbed a plate and joined them, her cheeks still flushed from her run. Even the sweat glowing from her forehead had a chic sheen to it.

"No green smoothies, or anything like that. Plain old bacon and eggs and whatever Aria's got going on in that bowl."

"I think we can make that palatable with some brown sugar, banana, nuts." Carly grabbed a glass and shoved it beneath the juice dispenser.

When they were all seated around a table near the window, Axel said, "Alana's working on getting that autopsy report for us and pulling some strings to accelerate the toxicology test on Mom and the DNA test on Mom and baby. The more we know about these women, outside of their fake IDs, the faster we're going to solve this case."

Carly looked up from slicing her banana into her oatmeal. "I'm going to be looking at the first victim's toxicology report today. If I have any questions about the opioids in her system, I'll hit you up, Aria."

"Sounds good. Axel and I are going to Jane Doe number two's crime site today, just to get a lay of the land." Aria dipped her spoon into the oatmeal and swirled the brown sugar into a ribbon through the sludge.

"I'm not late for breakfast, am I?" A tall woman who looked more like the supermodel Iman than an FBI liaison strode into the breakfast room, her dark curls bouncing at her shoulders. "I'm starving."

"Don't skip out on a team dinner next time," Axel scolded. "Come over here and meet our newest agent."

Rihanna Clark put her plate down and floated toward the table like a ballerina in *Swan Lake*.

"Oh, get your breakfast first." Aria flicked her fingers at Rihanna.

"The breakfast will still be there in two minutes. I feel bad about missing your first meeting." Rihanna flashed a smile at Aria that made her feel like her best friend in the world. "First things first. I'm Rihanna Clark."

Aria grabbed her extended hand and then loosened her grip on the delicate bones of Rihanna's fingers. "Aria Calletti. Nice to finally meet you."

"I know." Rihanna pouted, her lips turning down at the corners. "I missed the big meeting yesterday because I was settling the baby, and I missed the team dinner, as

Axel called it, because I had to do some follow-up with CPS after we dropped the baby off with the family."

"How *is* the baby?" Aria curled her fingers around her spoon so hard, it almost sprang from her grasp. The thought of him outside next to his dead mother squashed her appetite even more than her lumpy oatmeal.

"He seems healthy. Doesn't seem like he has drugs in his system, but the toxicology will tell. His foster parents are topnotch. No worries there. Poor little guy." Rihanna's dark eyes shimmered with tears.

"Go get breakfast. We're not going anywhere." Aria plunged her spoon into her untouched bowl of oatmeal.

"Speak for yourself." Axel stuffed the remainder of his eggs into his mouth, leaving the sausage on his plate, proving his choice wasn't much better than her own. "I have to sign for our rental car, which is being delivered to the hotel in a few minutes. Meet me out front when you're done with breakfast—no rush."

As he walked away, Carly said, "Axe is just like Alana. Even though he's the supervisor, he sees himself as one of us."

"He seems very…charming, personable. Those qualities must be invaluable as a negotiator and interrogator."

"He amazes me, given his…past." Carly shot Aria a look from the side of her eye.

"I know." Aria's knees bounced beneath the table. "We read about his background in the Academy, about the murder of his parents and brother when Axel was a child. How awful. I can't even imagine."

"Most people can't." Carly picked up her coffee cup, pinky in the air, and took a dainty sip.

"Oh, now I have to sit with the healthy oatmeal girls." Rihanna clicked down her plate, overflowing with eggs, bacon, sausage and hash browns. "And I put ketchup on everything."

Aria widened her eyes. "Doesn't everyone?"

"I knew I liked you." Rihanna jabbed her fork in the air at Aria.

Aria chatted with the two women while they finished breakfast. She then excused herself to meet Axel, with a detour to her hotel room to grab her bag and make sure she didn't have oatmeal stuck to her teeth.

When she exited the hotel, she spotted him behind the steering wheel of a dark blue sedan, nodding his head. Was he on speaker phone? Should she interrupt?

She approached the vehicle and peered through the glass, which was practically vibrating with the loud, thrashing rock music blaring from the car's speakers. She tapped on the window as she pulled open the passenger-side door.

Axel's head shot up and he cranked down the noise. "Sorry about that. Just getting into the mood. Do you like heavy metal?"

"Mmm, I'm more of a pop girl, top forty stuff, but I've been getting into classical lately. I find it soothing."

"I do, too. If you're just learning about classical, I can steer you to a couple of composers and forms—sonatas, concertos and symphonies. I have an extensive collection."

"But you like headbanger music, too."

"Yeah, there's a time to relax and a time to…not

relax." His jaw formed a hard line as he pressed the ignition button on the rental.

Axel drove to the location of the second murder and parked on the street above the gravel walkway along the lake. Aria followed Axel out, stumbling down a dirt pathway through the marshy land and tall grasses.

Her nose twitched at the scent of dark, dank peat. "Why would she be walking down here when there's that perfectly good Blue Water River Walk?"

"You're the drug czar. If she were selling, would she be doing that in a more populated area or out here in no-man's-land?"

"That depends." When they reached gravel road next to the water, Aria brushed off the wet grass clinging to her low-heeled boots. She threw her arm out to the side. "Plenty of places to hide. If the killer stalked her, he'd have cover."

"*If* he stalked her?"

"I mean, if he wasn't with her. She could've known him, been with him, come out here with him. Again, that would explain why he didn't harm the baby and how he got close enough to take that shot without any defensive moves on the victim's part." She sucked in her bottom lip. "She dropped where she stood, right? No evidence that she fought back or turned to run."

"Kind of hard to run carrying one of those car seats with a six-month-old baby inside. That's gotta add another twenty, thirty pounds to the load, right?" Axel spread his hands, as if he didn't have one clue about babies.

He probably didn't.

"Closer to twenty than thirty pounds, maybe a little less." She shrugged. "I'm no expert, but I do have nieces and nephews."

"That's more than I got."

Aria sealed her lips. She had a wealth of siblings while Axel had lost his only brother in the most tragic way imaginable.

The gravel crunched beneath Axel's feet and he stopped and closed his eyes. "If he took her by surprise, he wouldn't have followed her on this road—too noisy."

"Over here, close to the water." Aria trailed her hand along the tall grasses that bordered the lake's edge.

Still rooted to the ground, Axel pointed ahead. "Right there. That's where it happened."

Aria jerked up her head and narrowed her eyes at a piece of yellow crime scene tape with a jagged end dangling from a bush. Then her gaze tracked to the dark stain soaked into the dirt. "No rain yet to wash that away."

His mouth grim, Axel strode toward the site and circled the bloodstain. "The shot spattered the baby with blood, you know. Little red droplets interspersed with the pandas on his blue blanket."

Curling a hand around her throat, Aria swallowed. "I saw that picture."

"So, she knew him, came here with him, or he snuck up on her through the reeds and grasses. Bam! Shot her point-blank. Left the scene and called 9-1-1 in a fit of conscience or to show off his handiwork."

"Not a serial killer, though, not with the exact same IDs and the drugs." She cocked her head, and the ponytail she'd decided on today slipped over her shoulder. "Why do you think he left the scene before calling 9-1-1?"

"Give himself some time to hightail it out of here." Axel stuffed his hands inside his pockets. "What are you thinking, Aria?"

"Water all around this area. He could've had a boat. She could've had a boat. I keep coming back to the boats. He could've called from here and hopped in his boat. Maybe he even laid low and made sure the first responders showed up in the right place—for the sake of the baby."

"A real prince," Axel growled low in his throat.

Aria sidled up next to the bloodstain and pivoted toward the water. She glanced at the ground and the trampled grasses. Could've been the killer. Could've been the cops on the scene. A white scrap of paper had been caught on the side of one of reeds and she ducked through the grass to take a closer look.

"Axel, there's a tissue caught on a plant. The cops scanned the area for cigarette butts and all the rest, right?"

"They did." Axel hovered over her shoulder. "It could've tumbled in here after."

"Or they missed it. That tissue is awfully white and unsullied for being debris from the lake or the road above." She cranked her head over her shoulder. "Do you have an evidence bag on you?"

He patted the leather satchel strapped across his body. "I have a few in here. I even have some tweezers."

After scrambling through his bag, he handed her a plastic baggie and a pair of tweezers.

Aria crouched, used the tweezers to pluck the tissue from the reed and then dropped it into the baggie. She handed it to Axel. "We should drop that off at the PD. Detective Massey in the Major Crimes Unit, right?"

"Yeah, he's the lead. Good find, Aria."

They spent another thirty minutes at the site without any more aha moments, and then Axel drove to the Port Huron Police Department with their find.

Massey brought them back to his office and folded his tall, spare frame into the chair behind his desk. Aria wondered where he crammed his storklike legs. He toyed with the plastic-bagged tissue in his long, bony fingers. "I'm not trying to cover for my guys, but I don't think this was out there."

"It's breezy. It could've blown in after the fact."

Axel had enough experience to know, as FBI, you didn't ruffle the PD's feathers. You'd never get their co-operation when you needed it, if you did. Aria had been on the other end of that relationship with the FBI coming in and taking charge of cases. In some departments, there was no love lost between the PD and the Feds.

"Could be from our killer." Massey tapped the bag with his fingers. "We'll send it over to check for DNA. Did you find anything else out there?"

"No, just trying to get a sense of things. I'm going to go through the autopsy reports with Director Suzuki today. Did she get those?"

"She did. Delivered to the hotel this morning." Massey shuffled through a stack of papers at his elbow. "I do have something you might be interested in, something for you to check out when you have the time."

"We'll take anything and everything you have, Detective." Aria squared her shoulders. "I used to work as a beat cop in Detroit, and I know the leads can get overwhelming, especially as so many of them go nowhere."

"Detroit, huh?" Massey raised his gray eyebrows, which seemed to stick out at odd angles, giving him a surprised look. "Do you know Smitty? Lieutenant Gerald Smith?"

"I do know Lieutenant Smith. He was something of a mentor of mine."

Massey nodded, a smile cracking his lean face. "He always liked to take cops with promise under his wing."

"Great cop." Aria reveled in the warm glow of the room, comfortable knowing she was appreciated. Not only had she won the approval of Massey, Axel had bumped her knee.

The detective shook out a piece of paper he'd slid from the stack and pushed it across the desk toward her. "We took a missing persons report a few days ago about a young woman."

Aria glanced at the first few lines on the page for the missing woman—a Chloe Larsen. "This woman is about the right age as our victims, but she has blond hair and blue eyes."

"That's why we didn't connect it to the first victim and overlooked it for the second, but read a little farther down the report."

Axel leaned into her space as Aria ran her finger through the words. She sucked in a breath. "A baby. This is a missing persons report for a young woman and a seven-month-old baby, and CPS is telling us that the baby found with Jane Doe number two is between six and eight months. Despite the dissimilar physical descriptions, it's a big coincidence."

Axel jabbed his finger at the paper. "Too big to ignore. Who reported the woman missing?"

"A Gary Rhodes. He's working at the docks. You might be able to catch him on his lunch break, but give him a call first at the number on the report. He said something about not being disturbed at work."

Aria held up the report. "Can I take this?"

"Take it. We have a copy in our computer system."

Axel asked, "What is Gary Rhodes's relationship to the missing woman and baby?"

Massey steepled his fingers and stared at them over the tips. "Brother and uncle."

Chapter Four

When they pulled up at the hotel, Axel left the car running and scrambled out of the front seat. "It's all yours, Aria. Don't crash it."

"Too funny." She slid out of the car and walked around to the driver's side. "Let me know if you and Alana discover anything in the autopsies I should know. If this could be a match to Jane Doe number two, can I bring this Rhodes guy to the medical examiner's office to ID the vic?"

"Do it." Axel saluted, two fingers to his forehead that ended in a bow. "Good luck."

When Aria got in behind the wheel of the sedan, she adjusted the seat then squealed away from the hotel, laughing at Axel's raised fist in her rearview mirror.

Axel had put the address of the commercial dock in the car's GPS, and Aria followed the voice now. As she turned down the street that led to the parking lot, she slowed and entered the number from the report into her phone. It rang three times before flipping over to voice mail with a recorded robotic greeting.

At the beep, she said, "Mr. Rhodes, this is Special

Agent Calletti with the FBI. I'm calling about your missing persons report for a Chloe Larsen. I'm heading to the dock, so if you have a minute to talk to me on your lunch break, give me a call back."

She left her cell number and continued toward the dock. Instead of pulling into the parking lot, she rolled to a stop across the street.

She slumped in her seat and scanned through the photos she'd taken of the crime scene this morning. That was a lot of blood for one person to lose.

The phone rang in her hand and she checked the display before answering. He'd gotten back to her as soon as he could. "Special Agent Calletti."

"This is Gray... Gary Rhodes returning your call, Agent Calletti. Do you have news about my sister?" His voice, pitched low, had an urgent quality to it.

"Maybe. I'd like to ask you a few questions. Can I meet you at the dock?"

"Not a good idea, but I'm suddenly feeling ill. There's a diner on the other end of the docks, a marina where the pleasure boats are moored. Can you meet me there in half an hour?"

She didn't know why it wasn't a good idea to talk to him at work and didn't understand how he thought he was the one calling the shots, but she found herself agreeing to his proposal. "I'll find it. I have dark hair and I'm wearing a black coat with a purple scarf."

"Thanks." He ended the call before she could dictate any terms of her own.

She pulled away from the curb and curved around the dock to the end where people kept their boats and where there was a rental office. Would that office have a record of any boats rented out the night of the second victim's murder?

The diner sat back from the marina, a blue-and-white awning flapping over the front door and large windows eyeing the bay. She parked the rental on one side and entered the restaurant.

A hostess with shocking pink hair and a jewel gleaming in the side of her nose looked up from her phone. "One?"

"Two. The other person isn't here yet."

She swept her arm toward a couple of empty booths. "Sit anywhere."

Aria waited until a busboy finished clearing off a table by the window and then slid into the blue-vinyl banquette, which had definitely seen better days. The window gave her a view of the boats bobbing in their slips—and the little cottage that housed the rental office.

When the waiter moseyed by, Aria had to ask for two of everything. As she sipped her water, she glanced up from her phone every time the door to the diner opened with a jingle.

Finally, a single man strode through the door, running a hand through his collar-length, blond hair, his eyes scanning the room. When he settled on her, a little frisson of—recognition? Prescience? Pleasure?—tickled the back of her neck.

She had to cross her legs and grip the edge of the table to keep from jumping up to greet him. Apparently, Gary Rhodes's commanding presence affected other women in the diner in the same manner; quite a few pairs of eyes followed his progress across the room.

He reached her table and stuck out his hand. "Special Agent Calletti?"

"Yes." She placed her hand in his, the rough skin on his palm abrading hers. "Have a seat."

"Gary Rhodes." Scooting onto the bench seat across from her, he said, "Thanks for meeting me like this. I have my reasons."

She waited for those reasons but, instead of explaining himself, Rhodes grabbed the glass of water in front of him and downed half of it. "Sorry, busy morning at work."

"You must be hungry, too. Feel free to order lunch."

"I can't eat anything until I know what you have on Chloe." He hunkered forward, his strong, corded forearms braced on the Formica, his blue eyes, which matched the vinyl, sparking. The vitality of the man took over the table…and Aria. "Did you find a woman matching her description?"

"Not exactly. Chloe is your sister?"

His leg bounced beneath the table. "Yeah. My half sister."

That would explain the different last names, or maybe not. "Is Chloe married?"

"No." He took a deep breath, which expanded his chest beneath his blue work shirt, which also matched his eyes. "Why does this matter?"

"Just gathering information, Mr. Rhodes." She pulled a notepad and pen from her purse, so she could actually take notes instead of ogling Mr. Rhodes's physical assets. "You described your sister as five foot five, slim build, blond hair and blue eyes, correct?"

"That's right." He waved away the approaching waiter and he pivoted and left them alone. "Did you find her?"

"We didn't find a woman with that hair and eye color, but she did match your description in another way."

"She has a baby with her." He spread his hands on the table and drummed all ten of his fingers. "That's it, isn't it? You found a woman with a baby, a baby boy."

"We did. That's why the Port Huron Police Department turned your missing persons report over to us." Aria sipped her water to avoid meeting his intense gaze. She'd had to deliver bad news to victims' families before, and it never got easier, but for some reason she couldn't stand to look into this man's eyes, full of hope and cautious optimism.

"To us." Dragging his nails on the tabletop, he curled his hands into fists. "You're the FBI. I-is it drugs? Did you arrest her for drugs?"

Aria almost choked on her water. *His* Chloe was into drugs, too? She dabbed her lips with a napkin and raised her gaze to meet his. "We didn't arrest this woman, Mr. Rhodes. She's a murder victim."

The knuckles of his fists blanched and a muscle ticked at the corner of his mouth. "She's dead?"

"She is. Her body was found two nights ago, on a deserted gravel path next to the lake…"

"The baby?"

"He's safe. He's currently with Child Protective Services, although I think they've found him a foster home for now, until we can identify him…and the woman found next to his car seat."

Rhodes rolled his broad shoulders and cranked his head back and forth, as if resetting his course, or maybe preparing for the worst. "Did the car seat have toys attached to it? Some keys? A sheep?"

Did it? Were there keys? She was not going to devastate or give false hope to Mr. Rhodes on the basis of a set of plastic keys and a sheep. "I'm not sure. You asked about an arrest for drugs. Was Chloe involved with drugs?"

"Yeah, she was." With the tip of his finger, he traced a bead of water down the outside of his sweating glass. "She was addicted to opioids. Every time I read about an unintended overdose due to opioids, my heart stops. Are you sure this woman was murdered? Could it have been a drug overdose?"

"The victim was shot through the chest—and she's not the only one. There was another murder victim a few weeks ago in the same area, same scenario." She didn't have to tell him about the IDs or the drugs…not yet. "Was Chloe just a user or did she deal?"

"God, I don't know." He dug his fingers into his thick hair, ruffling the ends. "I think she may have sold some small quantities to finance her habit. She couldn't get money from me…for that. Anything she needed for herself or Danny, I bought. I didn't give her money because she'd spend it all on drugs."

Danny, the baby's name was Danny—if the victim was Chloe. Jane Doe number two had brown hair and brown eyes—but then, so did the other woman. The IDs indicated brown/brown.

"When did you realize Chloe was missing?"

"Just last week—Thanksgiving. She was supposed to come to my place for the holiday, told me specifically she'd be there, and then didn't show up."

"She's an addict."

"I know. That's why she usually blows off my invitations. If she has no intention of following through, she tells me flat-out." He ran his knuckles over the sexy reddish-blond stubble on his chin. "She told me she was coming for Thanksgiving, had a little money."

"She said that?" Aria scribbled in her notebook. She could've been dealing.

"Uh-huh."

The waiter crept up to the table again. "Are you going to order something?"

"Yeah, I'm sorry." Mr. Rhodes—Gary—picked up the laminated menu and ordered a cup of coffee.

Feeling sorry for the guy, Aria ordered a turkey sandwich on wheat, to go.

"How am I going to find out if this murder victim and baby are my sister and nephew?" His Adam's apple bobbed in his throat when he swallowed. "Do you have pictures?"

Aria didn't plan to whip out pictures of a dead body in the middle of a diner—even if she had them on her, which she didn't. "The victim's body is at the St. Clair County Medical Examiner's Office. I can take you there to ID the body."

The line of his jaw hardened, as if he were clenching his teeth. He gave one brisk nod. "I'll do that."

The waiter returned with Gary's coffee and a caddy of cream, sugar and fake sugar, placing everything on the table in front of him.

When the waiter left, Gary shoved the cup and saucer toward Aria and the dark liquid sloshed over the rim. "I don't want the coffee. I just felt like we should order something for taking up a table. Do you want it?"

"I felt the same way." She dumped some cream into the cup and swirled it through with a spoon. She didn't want it to go to waste, so she took a sip, wrinkling her nose.

Gary cocked his head. "You don't have to drink it if you don't want to."

"We never wasted anything in our house. If I don't drink at least half of this coffee, I'll have it put in a to-go cup." She brought the mug to her lips to hide her warm cheeks. She never got personal on the job. She had no idea what had made her spill embarrassing family habits.

"Frugality is not a bad quality to have." He drew shapes on the table with the tip of his finger. "Sometimes I think…never mind."

"Oh, come on. I revealed my family's extreme cheapness."

"I think if my family had had more qualities like prudence and self-awareness, maybe Chloe would've never gotten hooked on drugs. Having the best of everything without working for it, never denying yourself one single, thing—" he shrugged "—it's not a healthy way to live."

Aria sucked in the coffee too fast and it burned the roof of her mouth. She fanned her face as her gaze tracked over Gary's work clothes. The best of everything? Didn't this guy work at the docks?

She took a sip of water and rolled the glass between her palms. "Why'd we meet here instead of on the job? Your boss wouldn't have given you a few minutes to talk to the FBI about your missing sister?"

"I didn't want anyone to know I had a missing sister." He spread his hands, which had calluses but not the ground-in grit around his fingernails that most longshoremen accumulated after years on the docks.

Aria narrowed her eyes. "Why not?"

He lifted one shoulder. "I'm new on the job. I don't want the attention. I don't want my boss to think I'm not focused on my work."

Those were three reasons he gave her. Why did they all sound rehearsed? "So, you told your boss you weren't feeling well today."

"A little white lie." He leaned in close over the table. So close, she could smell his masculine scent, a mixture of soap and sweat. "Can you keep my secret, Agent Calletti?"

When he looked at her like that, like they shared a secret, special to just the two of them, she'd not only keep his secret, she'd swallow the key.

"We don't need to tell your boss." She ducked her head and reached for the coffee she didn't want, just to break away from his blue gaze that seemed to hold sway over her. "But if I'm going to be keeping your secrets, you'd better dispense with the agent business and call me Aria."

"Like a song from an Italian opera." He planted his elbow on the table and propped his chin on his fist. "I appreciate your…discretion."

Her heart fluttered in her chest like she had a crush on the high school football captain, who'd actually known better than to even look her way with her brothers standing guard. "If your sister does turn out to be this victim, you might not be able to keep your boss in the dark. You do have different last names, though."

"Chloe is my half sister. Same mother, different fathers and different last names." As the waiter dropped off her bagged sandwich, Gary said, "Anyway, thanks for meeting me here instead of barging onto the dock."

"No problem." She flipped open her wallet, pulled out a ten and three ones and anchored a bottle of ketchup on top of the bills.

Gary reached for his wallet. "I'll pay for the coffee."

"Taken care of. I'm not *that* cheap."

"Good to know." He pinched her bag of food between his fingers. "Can we get going now?"

Why was that good to know? It would only be good to know if they planned to see each other again, and they'd only see each other again if this Jane Doe turned out to be Chloe. She hoped fervently that wasn't the case and that she never saw Gary Rhodes again.

"You can follow me over." She slid from the booth and he followed suit, the bag dangling from his fingers.

He reached the door before she did and held it open

for her. They walked side by side to the parking lot. He pointed to a beat-up white truck. "That's me."

"I'm in the black sedan on the next row. I have the address to the medical examiner's office, so you can follow me over," she repeated. She stood in front of him awkwardly, tilting her head back, waiting for her sandwich. "You can keep that if you want."

"Oh." He blinked lashes way too long for a long-shoreman, and placed the bag in her hands as if it were precious cargo instead of a turkey sandwich. "I'll see you over there."

As she reached her own car, Aria mumbled to herself, "Don't turn around, don't turn around."

She did anyway and caught Gary next to his truck, looking after her.

He raised his hand and she did the same, as if just verifying with him that he knew which car belonged to her, instead of wanting to get one last look at him—before his world was possibly wrecked.

When she got in her car, she placed a call to the medical examiner's office to give them a heads-up. She recited the case number and let them know a possible family member was coming in for an ID.

With this knowledge, the morgue attendant would get the body out of the cooler. Nobody wanted to see his or her loved one being pulled from a drawer. They'd also cover the body with a sheet and just fold back the cover from the face.

As soon as she ended the call, another one came in from Axel. "Hi, Axel. I'm on my way to the ME's office with the brother tailing me. He confirmed his sister was into drugs and her baby is seven months old, but she is a blond-blue."

"Yeah, about that, Aria…" Axel cleared his throat. "I was looking over the autopsy reports with Alana, and Jane Doe number two doesn't actually have brown eyes."

Aria's gaze darted to the rearview mirror with Gary's beater on her tail, a sick churning in her gut.

"What does that mean, Axel? White female with brown hair and brown eyes—that's what we got."

"Jane Doe number two was wearing contacts—brown contacts."

Chapter Five

Grayson tried to keep up with the sedan in his rumbling truck. Didn't FBI agents have to be good drivers?

He ran his tongue along his teeth in his sandpaper mouth. That eight-ounce glass at the diner hadn't cut it. He needed about a gallon of water. He released his tight grip on the steering wheel and flexed his stiff fingers. Despite the chill outside, a bead of sweat ran down his back beneath his clothing.

This victim had brown hair and brown eyes. Chloe had blond hair, lighter than his own, and big blue eyes that used to sparkle when she was a little girl—before the bad choices and the drugs.

When Dad had died in a private plane crash and Mom had married Gunnar Larsen—too soon after Dad's death for Grayson's liking—he'd resented it. Had resented the stepfather who'd tried to replace Dad, who'd lived high on the hog on the money Dad had earned. But he never resented his little sister. He'd always protected her. But he'd gotten busy expanding Dad's business and Chloe had gotten wild after her own father had died on a drink- and drug-fueled binge.

Maybe Grayson hadn't done enough, but he'd make it up to Danny. If this poor woman, with brown hair and brown eyes, didn't turn out to be Chloe, once he found his sister, he'd do better for both her and her son.

How could this be Chloe, unless Agent Calletti was mistaken about the victim's description? Agent Calletti—Aria—didn't strike him as someone who made mistakes. Except when she drove.

Did she just roll through that stop sign? He tapped the brake pedal and accelerated after her. She put on her turn signal and he followed her into the parking lot of McLaren Port Huron hospital.

He was out of the truck before she exited her vehicle and waiting by her open car door as she collected her bag and purse from the back seat.

She seemed surprised to see him next to her car, as if she'd forgotten the purpose of this visit. He couldn't, and he shoved his unsteady hands into his pockets.

"Are they expecting us?"

"I called on the way over. I'll let hospital reception know we're here and on our way to the medical examiner's office, which is located in the hospital." Her coffee-colored eyes shimmered when she looked at him. Then she dropped her dark lashes to shutter them.

A feather of apprehension brushed the back of his neck. Did she realize she'd made a mistake about the coloring of the victim? He didn't want to put her on the spot in the middle of the parking lot, so he stiffened his spine and said, "I'm ready."

The hospital doors whispered open and Aria strode up to the reception desk and stated their business.

The receptionist, her lip-sticked mouth pinched into an *O*, slid a glance his way. He must look as bad as he felt. He licked his lips. It couldn't be Chloe. She had blue eyes.

"They're ready for us." Aria's low heels clicked on the linoleum as she walked to the elevator.

When the doors opened, a few people spilled out and Grayson smacked his hand against the door to hold it open for Aria.

As a man jogged up to squeeze in before the doors closed, Aria said, "We're going down."

"Oops." The man backed up and the doors trundled to close the two of them in the dark interior of the elevator.

Of course, the morgue would be in the basement. Cold, dim, isolated. Chloe didn't belong in a place like that.

The doors opened into a long hallway, one fluorescent light at the end flickering, giving the place a ghoulish atmosphere. He rolled his shoulders back. His imagination was working overtime down here.

Aria walked ahead of him, hardly moving fast, but his own footsteps trailed behind hers as if he had lead boots on his feet.

She stopped at a door with a window in the top, safety glass with embedded wire mesh. Aria was too short to see through the glass, but Grayson could make out a metal table with a body covered by a sheet on top of it. Pain stabbed his temple.

Aria touched his arm. "Do you want me to come in with you or wait here at first?"

He cranked his head toward her, widening his eyes. It never occurred to him that he'd have to do this alone. As the only person who knew about his fears except for the blasé police, Aria had to be with him in this. He had no one else.

Her hand still on his arm, she squeezed it. "I'll come in with you."

She rapped on the door with one knuckle and a man in blue scrubs and a blue tinge to his skin opened the door.

He nodded as he widened the door, his face grim, to match the company he kept in here.

The chill in the room didn't faze Grayson. His muscles had seized up as soon as they'd left the elevator, and his jaw ached from the clenching.

The attendant stood at the head of the metal gurney and Grayson looked at the form beneath the sheet for the first time. Chloe had more substance than that draped figure. She'd never been that tiny, had she?

"Are you ready, sir?"

Grayson swallowed the lump in his throat and nodded.

The attendant gingerly lifted the white sheet like a groom lifting his bride's wedding veil.

Grayson began shaking his head as he took in the white face with the brown hair scooped back from the forehead. It couldn't be Chloe…and then he saw the tiny mole, about a half an inch above the corner of her mouth. She used to call it her Marilyn Monroe mole to match her hair. Her hair. Brown hair. Chloe with brown hair.

"Gary?" Aria whispered his fake name, as if afraid to wake the sleeping girl on the ice-cold slab. "Is this Chloe?"

His nose stung and he sniffed. "Yes, that's her. That's my sister Chloe Larsen."

"I'm sorry for your loss, sir." The attendant flicked the sheet back over Chloe's face…and her mole.

Grayson's feet were rooted to the floor and the three of them stood around Chloe's body in a frozen tableau. He realized Aria and the morgue attendant were waiting for him—to scream, yell, cry, collapse? Probably just waiting for him to move so the guy could shove her back into that drawer.

Aria's hand brushed his; it was the only thing that felt warm and alive in here. "Do you want to leave, Gary?"

He peeled his tongue from the roof of his mouth and managed a sound in the back of his throat. He turned for the door with a stumble in his step and Aria caught his arm.

She yanked the door open and practically shoved him into the hallway.

He walked toward the elevator and then did a half turn and fell against the wall. He covered his face with one hand and uttered the one thing that had been keeping him going since the moment Aria had called him. "I didn't see her eyes. Her eyes were closed. Chloe has blue eyes."

"Gary—" Aria touched his shoulder "—Chloe was wearing brown contacts. And, as you saw, her hair was dyed brown."

His hand slipped from his face. "Why? The hair,

maybe, but why go through the trouble of wearing contact lenses to change your eye color?"

"There are a few things I didn't tell you about the case." She glanced over her shoulder at the door to the morgue. "Let's get out of here."

They didn't say a word to each other until they walked out of the hospital. Grayson filled his lungs with fresh air, taking several deep breaths. Chloe was dead. Murdered. He'd have to tell Mom…if he could find her. At this time of the year, she'd probably be in the Caribbean with her latest European *royal* boy toy.

Aria dragged some keys from her purse. "Let's sit in my car for a minute. Do you need some water? I can run back inside and get you something to drink from the vending machine."

Grayson grabbed the back of his neck and dug his fingers into his flesh. "I have some water in my truck. We can sit there. Do you need to let someone know I ID'd the…victim?"

"I'll send a text. You need to sit down."

Did he look like he was about to unravel? He needed to stay strong. He may not have always been there for Chloe in the past, but he planned to be there for her now. "I'm all right."

He led her to his truck and opened the passenger door for her. He placed a hand on her elbow as she stepped onto the running board and helped her inside the vehicle.

He went around to the other side and got in behind the wheel, reaching into the back for his lunch pail. He unzipped it and pulled out a bottle of water and a sandwich. Holding the food out to Aria, he said, "You didn't get a chance to eat. Have this."

"I'm not hungry. Are you all right? I'm so sorry for your loss. I know you never believed this woman was your sister until you looked at her face."

Closing his eyes, he chugged down the water. "It didn't even look like her, not really, not with the brown hair, and her face looked so...but I recognized the mole above her mouth. And once I saw that, I saw Chloe. But why the contacts? Why the hair color? What the hell is going on?"

"I mentioned the other victim to you—also brown hair and eyes. She and your sister looked very similar."

"Was that victim wearing contacts, too?"

"No, and her hair was naturally brown."

"What does it mean?"

"Both women were carrying identical IDs—same name, same physical description, same address."

Grayson squeezed the bottle of water with one hand, denting it. "What was the name on the ID?"

"Maddie Johnson. Does that mean anything to you?"

"No. Is she a real person?"

"Nothing about those IDs was real. The address was fake, too."

"Chloe wore brown contacts and dyed her hair to match this ID for some reason. Is there any other connection between my sister and the other woman?"

Aria pinned her hands between her knees, and her chest rose and fell quickly. "They both had packets of fentanyl on them—packaged to sell. The first victim also had opioids in her system, but the toxicology report on your sister hasn't come back yet."

Grayson slammed his hand against the steering wheel. "I knew it. This has something to do with drugs. She was using. She was selling. And she put Danny in danger. Where is he? Who has Danny? I need to see him."

"I told you before, Gary, Danny's with a foster family right now for his protection."

"Protection from me?" He jabbed his thumb against his chest as his blood heated. The shock and sadness that had hit him in the morgue were quickly morphing into anger—anger at Chloe, anger at her killer, their mother, himself. With the water bottle still gripped in his hand, he slammed it into the cup holder. "I'm his uncle. He doesn't need protection from me. I'm the one who's going to protect him from now on."

Aria watched him steadily, her dark eyes liquid pools of sympathy. "Look at it from the viewpoint of CPS. This baby escaped an encounter with death. CPS doesn't even know who his mother is right now. They don't know his father, and they don't know who you are. They can't allow some random guy to show up and claim the baby. You understand that, right?"

Her measured tone sounded like she was talking to some wild man who had to be talked off the ledge. His chest heated with shame. Aria didn't deserve his anger.

He tilted his head back against the headrest and drew in a long breath. "I'm sorry, Aria. I didn't mean to go off on you."

"Look, you don't have to apologize to me." She swept

her ponytail off her shoulder with one hand. "This has been a shock. I understand you're upset. You have every right to be upset, angry, howling at the moon."

"Not quite there yet." He ran a hand through his hair. "What do I need to do to prove I'm Danny's uncle? How can I get him back?"

"Our FBI liaison is working with CPS. I'll get in touch with her and let her know I've located the baby's uncle. The Port Huron PD already ordered a DNA test for Chloe and Danny to make sure they were mother and child. Once CPS has Danny's DNA, you'll probably be asked to submit yours for a match. Will there be a father involved?"

"I have no idea who Danny's father is. Chloe never told me—if she even knew." He crumpled his hand into a fist and pounded his chest. "I'm all he has now. Our mother is not interested in being a grandmother. I don't think she's even seen Danny once."

"Are…are you married?"

"No. Why do you ask? You don't think a single man can take care of a baby?" He folded his arms and glanced at her from the corner of his eye.

"I think it's difficult for a single man or woman to care for a baby, especially without experience…unless you have children." Her knee bounced up and down, and he almost placed a hand on her leg to stop it.

He dug his fingers into his biceps. "I don't have children, and you're right, I don't have any experience with babies. But I can take care of Danny."

"You'll need help." She held up her hand, flashing him a peace sign. "No offense, but I know what it's like to work long hours. As a longshoreman, you probably work long and physical hours. It's a lot to expect you to deal with a baby when you get home from work."

"I'm not a longshoreman, Aria. I'm here in Port Huron under false pretenses, and my name's not Gary. It's Grayson, Grayson Rhodes, and I'm going to find out who killed my sister."

Chapter Six

Aria whipped her head around to face him. That explained some things about the mysterious Mr. Rhodes, but not all. For all his outrage, was he mixed up in his sister's death?

"Whoa, back up. You've been lying to me?" She pressed her lips together in a hard line.

"Not about the important stuff. Chloe is my sister and Danny is my nephew." He plucked the misshapen plastic bottle from the cup holder and took a sip of water.

"How'd you wind up in Port Huron working at the docks under an assumed name—half assumed name?"

"When Chloe and Danny went missing and the cops didn't seem to give a rip, I figured I might be able to do some snooping around on my own. Chloe had mentioned hanging out around here, so I figured it was a good location to start. What better place to glean some information about a missing person near the border than at a dock, around boats?"

"So, you're undercover? That's why you don't want your boss to know about Chloe." Civilians working undercover never turned out well—even when the civilian was the very capable-looking Gary—Grayson. No longshoreman in the history of mankind was ever named Grayson.

She clicked the window button. "I need some air."

Grayson turned the key in the ignition and she buzzed down the window a few inches. The cold air that blasted into the truck hit her like a slap to the face—a second slap to the face. She was FBI now. Shouldn't she have figured out he really wasn't a longshoreman? The signs had been there. Axel would've made Grayson in about two minutes.

"That's right. I'm hoping to pick up some information. The ice there is just beginning to thaw."

She narrowed her eyes. "How'd you get that position so fast? Work at the docks is a prime job around here."

"I'm not taking a job away from anyone." He raised his right hand. "I swear. I know someone who knows someone in high places, and the opening was created for me—and I earn my keep. I'm no slacker."

Her gaze traveled across his wide shoulders and got caught on his solid biceps beneath his shirt. "Didn't say you were. Have you heard anything, yet?"

"No, but now that I know more details about the murders of Chloe and the other woman, I'll have a better idea of what to look out for." His blue eyes, as he stared over the top of the steering wheel, were chips of ice. "Are you going to rat me out to the cops or your FBI buddies?"

"The cops? No. My FBI *buddies*? Maybe. I'm the new kid on the block, and I don't want to start out my career by keeping secrets from my coworkers."

"I understand that, and I don't want to put you in a compromising position." He touched the back of her hand and drew back as if he'd received an electrical shock. "I want to thank you again for coming in there with me."

His touch acted like a prod and she almost jumped in her seat. "I—I had to be in there with you for the purposes of the identification."

"Not that. I know that." He held on to the steering wheel again with both hands, as if to anchor himself. "Having you there softened the blow. You knew it was Chloe before we walked in there, didn't you?"

"I had received a phone call from my supervisory agent, who'd been going over the autopsy reports, and he told me the victim had been wearing brown contacts. So, I knew her eyes were blue. Yes, I knew. I'm so sorry."

"It's still so unreal right now." He rubbed his knuckles across his scruff. "But I'm not giving up on finding Chloe's killer. I'm keeping that job on the docks."

"I'm not going to encourage you to investigate on your own, but I'm not going to stop you." She pulled her purse into her lap and inserted her fingers in a side pocket to pull out her business card. "I didn't even give you my card yet."

"I have your number in my phone from when you called me."

She dug in her purse for a pen and scribbled on the back of the card. Pinching the card between two fingers, she held it out to him. "My personal cell phone number…just in case."

As he reached for it, she yanked it away. "Are you going to tell me who you are? What made you come to Port Huron to look for Chloe? You're not from here."

"I live in Detroit. When my father died, he had left the majority of his business in trust for me. I was only eight when he passed away. My mother remarried a few years later and she and her new husband had Chloe. Chloe's dad died when she was a teen and then she spiraled out of control. My mother couldn't handle her, and I was busy building up my father's business." He pinched the bridge of his nose and squeezed his eyes closed.

She wanted to reach for him again, run her hand down his arm, soothe away his guilt, but that wasn't her job. The best way she could serve Grayson and Chloe was by catching her killer. "Chloe moved to Port Huron?"

"Chloe didn't move anywhere—she just moved around. Sometimes she'd tell me where she was and sometimes I didn't hear from her for months at a time. I knew about Danny, tried to send her things for the baby, things she couldn't hock for drugs." He twisted his head toward her when she'd made a sound in the back of her throat. "Yeah, it was that bad."

"How'd you know she was in Port Huron?"

"I invited her to my place for Thanksgiving, just like I always did, only this time she accepted. She rarely took me up on my invitations, but this time she agreed to come over. Told me she was in Port Huron for a job." He snorted, the nostrils of his patrician nose flaring. "I should've known what kind of job."

"Was Chloe ever involved in…sex work?" Aria bit her bottom lip.

"I don't know. I wondered if that's where the baby came from." His mouth tightened. "I hate to admit it, but it wouldn't surprise me if she was hooking. She had an expensive habit."

"So, she'd do anything for money, including sell drugs?"

"I think so. You found fentanyl on her, right? Enough to sell?"

"That, or she'd just made a buy."

"Question for you." Grayson braced his hands against the steering wheel. "Why didn't the person who killed her take the drugs off her? Why not take it to use or to sell or to point the finger in a different direction?"

"You're thinking like a cop. We're not sure, unless the drugs were left on the victims to make a point." Her cell phone rang and she held up her finger to Grayson. "I need to take this."

When she answered, and before she could even say hello, Rihanna started breathlessly talking into the phone. "I heard from Axel that you identified Jane Doe number two. Good work, Aria."

"I did." Aria's gaze slid to Grayson, staring out the window, a muscle twitching next to his eye. "She's Chloe Larsen, and her baby's name is Danny. I'm with her brother and the baby's uncle right now. He wants custody of the baby. The grandmother is out of the picture, and he's the nearest living relative."

Grayson nodded.

"That's great. Danny's a little love. His foster parents got him last night and adore him already." Rihanna lowered her voice as if Grayson could hear her over the phone. "Is the uncle prepared to give his DNA? We can't go handing this baby off to a random stranger. What's the uncle's name?"

"His name is Grayson Rhodes, and he's more than willing to have his DNA checked. He's anxious to get custody of Danny."

Grayson nodded again, more aggressively this time.

"Grayson Rhodes." Rihanna whistled. "I know that name."

"You do?" Aria's gaze darted to Grayson once more, now glancing through his phone.

"He's a hotshot developer in Detroit. His company is coming in and gentrifying whole blocks. The dead girl is Grayson Rhodes's sister?"

"I'll tell you about it later. When do you want Mr. Rhodes to submit his DNA and to whom?"

"I'll take charge of him—and if he looks anything like his pictures, I'll be more than happy to do so."

Two spots of heat flamed in Aria's cheeks. "I'll have him contact you. Thanks, Rihanna."

"Thank *you*, superstar."

Aria ended the call and cleared her throat. "I'm going to give you the number of our liaison with CPS. Her name is Rihanna Clark and she'll walk you through the DNA submission. The sooner they can verify you, the faster you'll get Danny."

"I just want him home for Christmas. Do you think that's possible?"

"You'll have to ask Rihanna, but I don't see why not."

She checked the time on her phone. "You should probably see if you can get that done while you're off work. I assume you're going back tomorrow."

"I know so much more now, thanks to you. I know what to listen for. I know what questions to ask."

"Don't show too much interest or you'll give yourself away."

He raised one eyebrow. "Thanks for the tip. You do much undercover work?"

"Believe it or not, I was a narc working in high schools." She smoothed her hands over her professional slacks.

"I can believe it—I mean the looks, not the attitude—unless you were the quiet girl who kept her mouth shut."

"That's exactly what I was, and I advise you to be the same type. Keep your eyes and ears open, but don't snoop around. You'll give yourself away." She dipped down to reach into her laptop case, feeling for Rihanna's cards. They all kept Rihanna's cards along with their own for moments like this. She snapped the card onto the console. "This is Rihanna Clark's info. I'll let you go now so you can take care of the DNA and not have to miss out on work."

"Thanks, Aria. I don't think I could've gotten through this without you today." He pointed to his smooshed sandwich on the console. "You can have that, if you want."

"I've got my own sandwich from the diner, remember?" Sitting across from him in the diner seemed like it happened a million years ago. "You eat it. You've had a shock."

"I don't feel like eating anything." He picked up the sandwich and let it drop. "Is food supposed to cure shock?"

"I'm Italian. Food cures everything." She smiled at him and her heart hurt for the pain in his blue eyes.

"Maybe later." He picked up Rihanna's card and held it up to the window, framing it with his fingers. "Is she expecting my call today?"

"If you explain your work situation and she's free, I'm sure she'd be happy to take you over this afternoon before the office closes."

"My work situation." He flicked the corner of the card. "I didn't hear you tell her I was here under false pretenses."

Aria coughed. "She recognized your name. She knows who you are."

"And you didn't?" He flattened out the card on his knee.

"Rihanna deals with the media all the time, so it makes sense that she'd know your name and company."

"Is she going to be willing to keep my name out of the news in regard to Chloe's murder? Once my cover is blown at the docks, I won't be able to sniff around there."

"I think she'll oblige you. We don't want too much getting out about these two murders just yet." She pulled the door handle and the door of the truck creaked as it swung open. "Are you okay?"

"No, but I'll do what I need to do now." One corner of his mouth lifted. "Thanks again for your help, Aria."

"You're welcome, of course. I didn't really do anything except bring you bad news, though."

"Bad news I needed to know."

She swung her legs from the truck and placed one booted foot on the runner, the other hanging in the air. "Call me if you do hear anything…and be careful."

"I will."

Hanging on to the truck, she slid to the ground and hiked her purse and laptop case on each shoulder as she walked to her car. This time she didn't turn around, but when she pulled out of the hospital parking lot she waved at Grayson sitting in his truck, his phone to his ear.

She drove back the hotel, her stomach rumbling with hunger. She parked in the hotel lot and ripped into the bag on the seat next to her. As she took a big bite of the turkey sandwich, she thumbed through her text messages. Apparently, Grayson's name hadn't rung any bells with Axel.

She also checked her personal cell phone and squeezed out a small breath when she saw a few texts from her family and no voice mails. Not that she expected Grayson to contact her immediately after talking to Rihanna.

She shouldn't expect Grayson to contact her at all, unless he had some information about the case. Rich guy slumming to catch his sister's killer. Did he think he was in some cheesy TV show?

She swallowed the last bite of the sandwich and dragged a napkin across her mouth. Then she bunched the paper bag in her fist and exited the car.

She made her way up to Alana's suite where the director had set up a temporary office. The Port Huron PD was in the process of clearing out one of its conference rooms for them, and Opaline was over there directing installation of the equipment they'd need for the case.

She brushed crumbs from her navy-blue slacks and tugged on her matching jacket. She'd taken note that the others had dressed down a little, so she'd play it by ear.

She knocked on the door and Alana swept it open. "Good work on ID'ing Jane Doe number two, Aria. Come on in here."

Aria ducked her head and lifted her hand at Axel and Selena. "I really didn't do anything except meet with Mr. Rhodes, who'd reported his sister missing. Until Axel let me know Chloe was wearing brown contacts, I wasn't even sure we had the right person, except for the baby—matched the age and sex of little Danny."

"Did he give you any information about his sister?" Axel wedged his foot on the edge of the coffee table, littered with soda cans, coffee cups and water bottles. "We'll have him come in for further questioning."

"I'm sure he's eager to give us any info we need, but he just started a new job and can't get away that easily."

"Even after the murder of his sister?" Selena reached across Axel's leg and grabbed a can.

"H-he doesn't want his work to know that was his sister."

"I get that." Selena blinked her dark lashes and gulped down some soda. "We can make other arrangements for him. What's he going to do about his nephew?"

"Oh, he wants custody. I already put him in touch with Rihanna for a DNA sample. Says he wants him home for Christmas."

"That's sweet." Axel drilled a finger in the side of his cheek. "Is he a suspect?"

Aria's mouth dropped open. "A suspect? Wait. What? In the murder of his sister?"

"He's the closest one to her. We work outward." He drew ever-widening circles in the air. "We need to eliminate him."

"He reported her missing." Aria felt her voice rise in indignation and sealed her lips. Axel was right. They should look at close family as suspects. She'd been blinded by her sympathy for Grayson. Still, her gut told her he wasn't involved and she'd been right to trust him.

Axel didn't seem to notice her passion as he replied, "Killers report their victims missing all the time to pretend they didn't know they were already dead. What was his demeanor?"

"In denial when I told him the Jane Doe had brown hair and eyes. Couldn't believe it was her, but thought the baby with her was too much of a coincidence. When he saw her in the morgue, he was shocked, upset, got angry later. Just what you'd expect. I doubt he has a motive to kill his sister *and* some other woman who happens to have the same phony ID. He did say Chloe had an addiction and it wouldn't be out of character for her to sell drugs or turn tricks to indulge her habit."

Selena raised her eyebrows. "You spent a lot of time with this guy, huh?"

"I—we met in a diner to discuss his missing persons report, and then we drove to the morgue at the hospital…separately, to ID the body. I couldn't just leave him after that. He was upset and he had questions about Danny."

Alana looked up from her laptop. "You handled it perfectly, Aria, and I agree with you. He doesn't seem like a suspect, but Axel will perform his due diligence to rule him out."

Axel winked at her. "Still waiting on the toxicology tests for Chloe Larsen, but I'm not expecting a different result from the first victim's if the brother told you she was using."

"Obviously, Chloe was wearing brown contacts and dyed her hair brown to fit the description on the ID. The first victim already had brown eyes—no contacts—and maybe brown hair." Selena stood and walked across the room. She snagged a plastic bag and waved it in the air. "Who wants to help me clean up this mess? I'm looking at you, Axel."

"I will absolutely help, but now I know why Max hightailed it out of here."

"I'm going to shoo all of you out of here in a minute. I'm having dinner in my room, and I'm going to turn in early." Alana removed her glasses and rubbed her eyes. "We should have our command center set up by tomorrow at the PD, so report there in the morning after breakfast unless you have somewhere else to be."

Dinner alone and an early bed sounded good, but

Aria didn't want to miss out on any team time. "Is anyone else planning anything for dinner?"

Axel held up his fingers and ticked them off with each name. "Opaline's going to be busy setting us up for tomorrow, and Amanda just went over before you got here to help her. Rihanna is meeting a friend for dinner after she takes care of Rhodes's DNA test. Max is out for a marathon workout. Carly's running down some leads on the fentanyl found on the victims. Who'd I miss?"

"Me." Selena swung a full bag of trash from her fingertips. "I'm hanging out with Blanca. We have some training to do, and Axel's helping me. You're welcome to join us, Aria."

"You know, I think I'll head back to my room, order room service and put my notes in my laptop." Aria patted the side of her bag. "Do you need help with the cleanup in here?"

"You didn't even contribute to the mess." Selena flicked her fingers at the door. "Go—and take a can of soda with you." She pressed a cold, wet can into Aria's hand.

When she got back to her room, Aria realized she hadn't had anything to drink since that horrible coffee at the diner. She popped the tab on the soda and downed half of it before coming up for air, her nose tingling with the carbonation.

After transferring her notes from her meeting with Grayson into a file on her computer, she ordered fish and chips, coleslaw and a small bottle of chardonnay from room service and changed into a pair of sweats and an FBI T-shirt.

While finishing off her meal, Aria's personal cell buzzed. She licked the ketchup off her fingers, squished a napkin in her hand and tapped the display to read the text.

Her heart stuttered when she saw Grayson's name. She pushed away the tray and picked up the phone between her palms. She read the text: Gave my DNA. Couldn't see Danny.

She wiped her hands thoroughly and texted back, You will. Be patient.

She watched the blinking cursor in the text field for several seconds and then took a swig of wine. Maybe she shouldn't have responded so quickly.

When the words blurred before her eyes, she set the phone on the nightstand and hoisted her tray from the bed. She placed it outside the door of her room.

Grabbing her half glass of wine, she settled on the bed and turned on the TV. Another glance at her phone told her Grayson hadn't responded to her eager reply.

The wine or the TV must've lulled Aria to sleep because she woke with a start, her heart pounding. Then she bolted upright at the sharp knock on the door.

"Aria, are you awake?" Carly's voice on the other side of the door, low and urgent, had Aria scrambling from the bed. She pressed her eye to the peephole and pulled the door open.

Carly, in a pair of leopard-print PJs, her face as pale as her hair, folded her arms and said, "Alana got the call. We have another one."

"Another one?" Aria shook her head, dislodging the wisps of sleep clinging to her sluggish brain.

"Another murder of a brown-haired, brown-eyed girl."

Chapter Seven

Alana shoved her gloved hands into her coat pockets and puffed out a breath, watching it form in the cold air. Her boots crunched the gravel as she moved toward the bright lights illuminating the crime scene, the body crumpled on the ground, little numbered cones scattered around the victim, a young cop unfurling a roll of crime scene tape.

With the Port Huron PD already out here, Alana had sent just Aria, Carly and Axel from the team—Axel to interface with Detective Massey from the Major Crimes Unit, Aria and Carly to remind the PD who was really in charge.

Aria didn't want to step on any toes, though. An FBI agent could get a lot more information if the PD felt it was working with you, not in competition with you. She'd seen it enough on the other side.

She approached Massey with her hand outstretched. "Detective Massey. We hit pay dirt with that missing person's report from Mr. Rhodes. Good instincts there. At least we've identified one of these victims, and maybe your department can help us ID this one, as well."

Running a hand over his thinning gray hair, trying to adjust it over his bald spot, a move he probably did subconsciously, Massey nodded at her. "Damn shame. I have two daughters around the same age. Makes me sick. Don't ever get used to it, Agent Calletti. If it still tortures you every night, you haven't lost your humanity."

Axel took a step in their direction, stopped and pivoted, leaving Massey to her.

"That's what Smitty used to tell me, sir." She circled the body, her finger ringing the air. "This looks a little different from the other two, doesn't it? The first two victims were flat on their backs, probably blown back from the blast of the gun. This one is on her side, scuff and drag marks in the gravel around her body."

Massey's shaggy gray eyebrows furrowed over his nose. "Like there was some kind of struggle."

"He either surprised the other two or they knew him. This time it looks like there was a tussle."

"Thank God, no baby with this one." Massey, grabbed one of the uniformed officers by the sleeve. "Pressler, make sure the victim's hands are bagged before the medical examiner gets here."

"Who found the body? No mysterious call this time?" Aria crouched beside the victim and eyed her dark roots. Another dye job?

"It was a jogger. Everything else the same, though. Same ID as the other two, and a quantity of fentanyl tucked in her purse, ready for sale." Massey cupped a hand over his mouth and yelled, "Make sure you do a thorough search this time. Agent Calletti found a tissue near victim two's crime site that we missed. Don't miss anything."

After several more minutes with Massey, Aria stepped away from him in case Max wanted an opportunity to talk to the PHPD detective. "Thanks for your help, Detective Massey."

She wandered over to where Carly was examining an evidence bag containing the baggie of fentanyl found on the latest victim.

Carly said, "Thanks to you, Aria, I'm having all the fentanyl tested for its purity and makeup. Maybe we can track where it's coming from."

Axel sidled up and wedged himself between them, ducking his head. "And thanks to Aria, we have a great relationship with the PHPD. She has gruff old Detective Massey over there eating out of her hand."

Aria opened her mouth to protest that it was just because they both knew Smitty, but she snapped it shut when Carly squeezed her arm. Why not take a little credit? She couldn't be the starstruck fan-girl her entire career with the FBI.

Instead she allowed a tiny smile to curl her lips— until she caught sight of the victim lying on the ground, a dark pool of blood at her back.

She wasn't here to score points. She was here to find a killer—and as Massey said, you never wanted to lose your humanity.

That woman was someone's daughter, wife…sister.

GRAYSON STUFFED A sandwich into his lunch pail and grabbed a bottle of water from the fridge. His current abode was one of those pay-by-the-week motels a few blocks from the lake—only the finest.

He'd spit into a tube yesterday to prove he was related to Danny. He'd do a lot more than that for the little guy if he could. He wanted that baby home for Christmas, wanted to give him the kind of life Chloe couldn't.

He'd tried to reach Mom last night, but she hadn't picked up. Probably didn't even have international calling on her phone in Mustique or wherever she was this time.

He'd almost texted Aria back after their exchange last night. Some need had driven him to let her know he'd supplied his DNA to CPS, but when she'd responded by advising him to be patient regarding seeing Danny, he felt like he'd whined enough to her.

Aria was typically the kind of woman he wined and dined and spoiled—at least in the looks department. But her demeanor couldn't be more different from the women he usually dated. He had a feeling Aria wouldn't be impressed by expensive bottles of champagne, a weekend in Paris or a Tiffany bracelet as a lovely parting gift.

He snorted and slammed the lid of his lunch pail. Why was he thinking about dating the serious FBI agent, anyway? She probably had a hard-nosed, nononsense cop husband or something and two kids. The fact that she didn't wear a wedding ring meant nothing.

As he unhitched his coat from the hook by the door, his phone buzzed. He glanced at the display, and his pulse picked up speed. Agent Calletti's ears must've been ringing.

"Hello?"

"Grayson, it's Special Agent Calletti… Aria. How are you doing this morning?"

"What are those stages of grief? I'm through the shock and denial, still feeling the guilt, and now I'm on the verge of white-hot anger—and I'm going to stay there until Chloe's killer is brought to justice."

"I—I have some news for you. Maybe you've seen it on TV already."

"Have you arrested someone? Did you find more evidence?"

"Another young woman was murdered last night." She rushed her next words as he absorbed this new shock. "Same MO—one shot to the chest, brunette carrying fentanyl and with the same ID as Chloe and the other woman."

Grayson gritted his teeth. "Another one. What the hell is going on, Aria?"

"We don't know yet, Grayson, but we're going to figure it out. The drugs and the IDs link these women, and being this close to the border, I'm betting the murders are connected to the drug trade."

He heard voices in the background as she said, "I have to get going, but I wanted to let you know about this murder."

"Thanks for keeping me informed. It means a lot."

They ended the call and Grayson charged out the door of his room, stuffing his arms into his jacket. The cops and the FBI agents weren't the only ones who were going to get to the bottom of this.

He needed to start making some friends on the dock.

AT THE END of the workday, Grayson punched his card in the time clock with the cracked face and jammed it into the slot on the wall. He said to everyone and no one in particular, "Helluva day. That one load nearly broke my back."

"C'mon, Gary. You're a big boy. You can handle it." Will, a beefy redhead with freckled arms, cackled.

"Yeah, seemed to me Gary was handling most of that load, Will, while you were sitting on your backside." Chuck punched his own timecard and winked at Grayson. "We're heading to The Tavern tonight for some beers. Wanna come this time? Did your landlord fix that toilet?"

"Yeah, he did, but it was kinda like Will here. He sat on his ass while I did most of the work." Grayson smacked Will on the back and the redhead let out his annoying laugh again. "The Tavern's the place near the noncommercial dock side?"

"That's it. They do a happy hour with half-price beers and some decent bar food." Will slung his jacket over his shoulder. "Just don't drink and drive in this town. I already got one deuce. The cops are real jerks about it."

"Got it. My place isn't that far if I have to walk."

Will elbowed Grayson in the ribs. "I'm hoping to get lucky with one of those pretty young things that flutter around the boats."

Grayson's breath hitched in his throat. "Oh, yeah? Do they hang out at The Tavern?"

"That, they do, my man. That, they do."

One of the younger guys yelled back, "Yeah, Will's been trying to hook one of them for years."

"Never give up." Will held up his index finger and then swapped it for his middle finger as he trudged to his truck.

Grayson headed for his own truck with his blood fizzing. Could the young women who hung around the pleasure boat dock and The Tavern be the ones involved in the drug trade?

Like a caravan, the work trucks pulled out of the parking lot and wended their way around the marina on the other side. Grayson followed along, glancing at the diner where he'd met Aria yesterday. He hadn't heard anything from her today but hoped the third victim had provided more evidence.

As his coworkers pulled their vehicles to the front of the bar, Grayson parked at the edge of the parking lot— better for a quick getaway. He dropped his phone into his pocket, leaving it on vibrate, and slid from the truck.

As he entered The Tavern, classic rock music thumped in his chest and several TVs silently broadcast sports channels, giving a blue glow to the dim interior. Grayson squinted toward the bar and didn't have to guess at the drink of choice as the place reeked of beer. The smell of it seemed to emanate from the walls, the wood floor and the pores of the clientele.

The dockworkers occupied most of the seats at the bar and a couple of them had wandered to the back room where the crack of pool balls dominated. Grayson made his way to Chuck and Will, bellied up to the bar, two longnecks in front of them.

Grayson ordered a round for the three of them and knocked back half the brew before wiping his mouth on his sleeve and grabbing a menu from between two napkin holders. "What's good?"

Chuck lifted one big shoulder. "The nachos. The wings."

Two young guys from the dock pushed their way to the edge of the bar and the dark-haired one smacked his hand on the sticky surface. "Chili cheese fries, Trevor."

The bartender flicked a white towel over his shoulder and wedged his hands on the bar, his tattoos snaking up one pumped-up arm in a multicolored sleeve. "Wait your turn, dude. Your uncle hasn't ordered yet."

Grayson's gaze flickered over the dark-haired, olive-skinned, twenty-something who'd demanded the fries—Tony something—and Chuck's ruddy face.

Chuck twisted his mouth. "My sister's kid, Tony Balducci. Pain in my big hairy backside. He works with us, although if you blinked, you'd miss it."

Tony laughed, his dark eyes turning into slits. "C'mon, Uncle Chuck. That job's just a temporary for me. I got me some bigger, better plans."

Chuck rolled his eyes. "Kid thinks he's gonna be a rap star. Anyway, bring us some wings and nachos, Trevor, and hell, bring out the chili cheese fries for Tony and Zane."

Grayson had seen Zane around the docks, too. With

his pimply neck and skinny arms, the kid didn't do any heavy lifting.

Zane held out his fist, a different letter on each finger before the first joint, for a bump with Chuck's. "You're the man, Uncle Chuck."

With a quick glance at the letters, Grayson could make out B-A-L-E-R. Was that supposed to spell baller? Clearly, Zane was a genius.

"Bring on the hotties." Will tipped his bottle toward the door at two young women sashaying into the bar, their heads together, both brunettes—or, one brunette and the other a raven-black.

Grayson's heart thumped in his chest. Could these two be involved in whatever was going down at the lake? A lot of women had brown hair, but he held up his phone anyway, peering at it and aiming it at the women. He snapped a few pictures.

As Will leaned in to see his view, Grayson switched to text. "Damn, ex-wife is texting me again."

"Put that number on ignore, dude." Will rapped his knuckles on top of the bar.

Grayson slid the phone into his pocket and finished his beer. "Who's ready for another round?"

"You got the last one." Chuck waved at Trevor. "It's my turn."

Two other guys from work joined them and they all proceeded to buy rounds of drinks until Grayson had three bottles lined up in front of him. He couldn't refuse. He also couldn't drink all that beer and expect to do any digging.

To Grayson's advantage, The Tavern got more and

more crowded, filling up with the after-work and boating crowds. The number of people gathered around tables and standing at the bar afforded him some cover.

When he saw the two dark-haired women make a beeline for the poolroom, he pushed away from the bar with a full bottle of beer in his hand. Might as well try to leave this somewhere. "I gotta hit the head."

As soon as he peeled away from the bar, another guy filled his place. Clutching his bottle by the neck, Grayson squeezed through clutches of people on his way to the poolroom.

He stepped just inside, propping up the wall with his shoulder, pretending to watch the action at the tables.

The two women he'd spotted earlier seemed to be waiting for the table where Tony and Zane were making ineffectual stabs at the stripes and solids, their beer bottles balanced on the edge of the felt.

Grayson narrowed his eyes as one of the women, dressed in a short denim skirt with knee-high boots, tugged on Tony's sleeve. He shook her off and wiped his nose with the back of his hand.

She backed off and leaned against the wall, her arms folded, her hands picking at the sleeves of her fringed jacket, the toe of her boot tapping.

Grayson had seen that same restlessness on his sister when she'd been jonesing for a high.

The game ended and the black-haired woman in jeans shrugged off her purple, fake-fur jacket and dropped it on a chair as she took the cue stick from Tony.

Tony then turned his attention to the nervous woman

in the skirt. He grabbed her upper arm and yanked her in his wake as he stalked across the poolroom.

Grayson turned to the sign-up sheet next to the door and bent over it.

When Tony and the woman spilled into the bar, Grayson straightened and poked his head out of the room. Tony was charging toward the back hallway of the bar, pushing the woman in front of him.

Grayson, keeping his head down, followed them. Were they going into one of the bathrooms? Maybe this was nothing more than a quick hookup.

Then Tony continued past the restrooms, toward the red exit sign glowing at the end of the hallway, and pushed the silver release handle, shoving the back door open.

Grayson flattened himself against the wall and inched his way down the hall. He couldn't charge out the back door without Tony noticing…but he could go outside from the front door and make his way around back. He drilled his bottle into the dirt of a potted plant where the hallway opened to the bar and weaved through the crowd to get to the front.

As he stepped outside, he turned to two women several feet away from the entrance, huddled into their jackets, puffing on cigarettes.

He asked one of the women, her red lips puckered as she blew out a stream of smoke, "Can I bum a smoke and a light?"

Her black-lined eyes widened. "Sure, handsome. Can I bum your phone number?"

Grayson chuckled. "Got a girlfriend."

"I bet she doesn't let you smoke." She shook a cigarette from her pack and pressed a book of matches from The Tavern into his palm. "I'd let you smoke. I'd let you do whatever you wanted."

"Thanks, ladies. Have a good night."

He cupped the cigarette and matchbook in his hand as he veered around the corner of the building. He slowed when he got to the back and hugged the clapboard as he crept toward a Dumpster behind the bar, his ears perking up at the sound of voices—one low, one high.

He crouched, pressing himself against the cold metal of the trash bin. The woman's voice floated toward him first.

"But what happened to them? Why were they killed?"

Grayson's heart thundered in his chest so hard, he was afraid it would pound against the metal and give him away.

Tony's voice, gruff like a wannabe gangster's, answered her. "You don't have to worry about that, Brandy. You don't get greedy. They got greedy."

"What do you mean? They just did what they were told to do."

"They didn't."

Brandy gave a squeak of pain, and Grayson balled his fists. *Coward.*

"What about the rest of us? What about me? I'm scared."

"You don't got nothin' to be scared of."

"Wh-what does that mean? How do you know that, Tony?" She gasped. "You didn't…"

"Shut your damn mouth. Those blah boaties got what was comin' to 'em. You keep your mouth shut and you take care of business, or you'll get what's comin' to you."

Brandy sobbed. "But the other girls, the baby…"

"Shut it!" A slap resounded in the crisp air. "That baby didn't get hurt 'cuz he didn't do nothin'. And if you don't do nothin', you won't get hurt, either."

Chapter Eight

Grayson clamped his teeth together against the sour bile rising from his gut. Tony killed Chloe. He knew it. He could take the bastard out right now and the world would be a better place.

A swell of music filled the alleyway and a rectangle of yellow light spilled onto the ground as someone opened the back door of The Tavern.

"What the hell? You two makin' out, out here?"

"Shut up, Zane. This is business."

"All right, all right, man. Rita's lookin' for Brandy, that's all."

"I'm coming." Brandy sniffed and the heels of her boots clicked on the asphalt.

Grayson bent forward and slipped around the corner of the building. He braced his hand against the wall for several seconds as he took deep breaths, calming his rage. "Blah boaties"? That's what they called these young women? His sister?

He'd tell Aria, but he had no proof. He couldn't have recorded that conversation from so far away. But he could get a picture of that animal.

With unsteady hands, he lit the cigarette and took a long drag. Better have a reason for stepping outside. He continued to smoke the cigarette as he returned to the front of the bar.

After a few more puffs, he ground out the smoke in the ashtray and returned inside. The noise level had increased a few more decibels since he'd left, and he wended his way back to Chuck and Will at the bar.

"Where'd you go?" Chuck shoved a beer at Grayson. "You have some catching up to do."

Grayson held out the matches between his two fingers. "Fell off the wagon and had to go out for a smoke."

Will waved a hand in front of his face. "You smell like an ashtray, dude. You'll never get the ladies that way."

"Unless the ladies are smokers." Grayson tilted back his head and poured some beer down his throat.

Chuck yelled across the room, "Hey, your chili cheese fries were getting soggy. We had to eat half of them."

Grayson's head snapped around and his adrenaline coursed through his veins as he watched Tony saunter across the bar, his arm casually slung around the shoulders of the woman he'd just assaulted and threatened in the alley.

Brandy, her eyes wide and her hair a tangled mess, wriggled away from Tony and turned back toward the restrooms.

Tony sidled up next to his uncle and dug his fingers into the sloppy fries, scooping up a handful. He shoved them into his mouth, congealed cheese hanging off the edge of his chin.

Tony plucked several napkins from the dispenser and wiped his face. He leaned over the bar, balled up the napkins and tossed them into the trash. He then grabbed another napkin and blew his nose.

Grayson traced his fingers around the edge of the phone in his pocket, barely breathing.

Tony stuffed the napkin he'd used on his nose into his pocket and picked up his beer. He gulped it down and placed the half-full bottle back on the bar, tilting his head to watch the TV above the bar.

"This better not be the ex, again." Grayson pulled his phone out, held it in front of him as if reading a text, and snapped two quick pics of Tony.

"I told you, man. You need to block that number." Will smacked him on the back. "Ready for another round?"

Grayson held up his bottle. "I'm good."

Zane stumbled up to Tony. "You ready to bounce? I wanna go home and play Fortnite."

"Yeah, I'm done with this place." Tony dug into his pocket and pulled out several bunched-up bills. He smashed them in front of Chuck. "Here's for the fries, Uncle Chuck, and a few of those beers. Gotta take care of family."

Grabbing a fistful of Zane's jacket, he hustled him out of the bar.

Chuck flattened the bills, ironing them with the side of his thumb. "Good kid. Always takes care of his family."

Yeah, you just have to worry if you're not in his family.

"That's good to see." Grayson corralled several bottles, including Tony's latest, and nudged them toward the inside edge of the bar. Then he grabbed a napkin and picked up Tony's bottle by the neck.

"I'm gonna hit the road." He tipped the bottle toward his group of coworkers. "Catch you tomorrow."

"Don't let the cops see you with that open container in your car." Chuck pinged the bottle with his dirt-encrusted fingernail.

"I'll finish it off before I get in the truck. Don't wanna waste it."

The bottle hanging from his fingers at his side, Grayson turned and almost bumped into Brandy, her makeup and hair repaired. She started to back away from him and he cupped her elbow, leaning close. "Are you okay? Do you need help?"

Her dark eyes widened for a second and she shook her head. Then she pivoted and scurried to her raven-haired friend.

Stepping outside, Grayson took a couple of deep breaths. What the hell was a blah boatie? "Blah" because they all looked alike? The cash, the threat to Brandy, the knowledge about Danny—if Tony Balducci wasn't the killer, he was involved up to his eyeballs.

When Grayson reached his truck, he tipped the bottle, pouring the beer onto the asphalt of the parking lot. He ducked inside his truck and tucked the bottle into his lunch pail.

He had Tony's fingerprints, DNA and picture. Even if

the FBI had only his word that Tony threatened Brandy and talked about dead blah boaties, they could still check this guy out. They must have some evidence at the crime scenes that could link the killer to his victims—Chloe.

He withdrew his phone and, cupping it in his hand, tapped his photos. Brandy, her long brown hair hanging over one shoulder, her arm through her friend's as they walked into the bar, could pass for Chloe. Grayson half closed his eyes and, through the blur, either woman could pass for Chloe, except for the darker hair of Brandy's friend.

Was the other young woman... Rita...was she a blah boatie, too? If she was, she didn't seem as worried about the murders as Brandy—if she knew about them. Maybe she was Chloe's replacement and was just waiting for her dye job.

He swiped his finger to the left to study the next picture. Tony didn't look like a monster. He had a soft spot for family. Is that why he'd spared Danny?

Grayson switched to his contacts and stared at Aria's number for a good ten seconds before tapping her initials, AC. He had information and he needed to give it to her.

She picked up after two rings. "Hello?"

"It's Grayson Rhodes. Sorry to disturb you this late, but I heard something I think you need to know."

"Okay."

"Are you busy?"

"I—I'm not. Just finished a working dinner." She paused. "Can you tell me what you heard?"

"Not over the phone." He rushed on. "I have something to give you, also."

"Can you come to my hotel?"

"I don't want to be seen there, just in case. I'm sure there are hotel employees who know who you are and why you're there. Those employees might know someone at the docks. I might be paranoid…"

"Not at all. You've put yourself in a precarious position. Where should I meet you?"

"I'm staying at a motel off the 25. The St. Clair Motel, room sixteen on the first floor."

"Got it. I'll be right over."

Aria ended the call and Grayson cranked on the truck. After a few sputters, the engine rumbled and Grayson pulled out of The Tavern's parking lot.

Could this information have waited for tomorrow? He gripped the wheel and punched the accelerator. Maybe the information could, but he didn't want to wait one more day to see Aria Calletti.

ARIA SPOTTED GRAYSON'S truck in the parking lot of the St. Clair Motel or the "St. lair Moel," according the partially burned-out sign. As she got out of the rental, the smell of fish choked the air and a brisk breeze off the lake stung her cheeks.

She pulled up her purple scarf and nestled her chin in the fuzzy folds. What could Grayson have discovered about the case? At least he was definitely off their suspect list. Axel had looked into his background and his whereabouts when Chloe had been murdered. Grayson was in the clear.

Still, was it guilt driving him? He didn't have to feel guilty about Chloe. He should know by now an addict couldn't be forced into recovery unless she was good and ready.

When Dad had gotten laid off at the auto plant, he'd hit the bottle pretty hard. There was nothing Mom, or any of them, could have done to make him stop. He'd had to go down that road himself. His DUI had finally woken him up; he'd started attending AA meetings. His younger sister had been killed by a drunk driver and his arrest for drunk driving had been the slap in the face he'd needed—his own rock bottom.

A couple of figures huddled in the shadows near the motel's office, and Aria rested her hand on her purse where her 9mm SIG-Sauer nestled. Grayson couldn't have found a better area? He probably could've purchased an entire motel out here.

She'd done a little internet searching and the guy was loaded. He'd expanded and solidified the real-estate development company he'd taken over from his father's partner. No wonder he was confident he could take care of his nephew. Men like Grayson had all the confidence in the world.

She made a wide berth around the two men, who were passing a paper-bag-wrapped bottle between them, and strode along the rooms bordering the gravel parking lot until she found sixteen, lights glowing from the front windows.

Leaning in close, she tapped on the door with one knuckle. She jumped back when Grayson swung open the door.

"Thanks for coming." He ushered her into the room with a sweep of his arm. "Sorry for the meeting place. Did those guys sharing the bottle bother you?"

She patted her purse. "They didn't, but I could handle them."

"Yeah, of course." He snapped the door closed behind them and slid the chain into place.

"What did you discover and how did you discover it?" Might as well make it perfectly clear she'd rushed out here to see him in the middle of the night for any light he could shed on the case—not because she'd been thinking about him on and off all day.

He wiped his hands on the thighs of his faded jeans. "I think I know who killed Chloe and the other women."

Aria felt her eyes bugging out of her head, not her most attractive look, but purely authentic. "You found out the killer? How? Who is it?"

"Can I start from the beginning? I want to lay this all out for you." He patted the back cushion of a worn sofa. "Have a seat."

She placed her purse next to Grayson's cell phone on the coffee table, scars crisscrossing the wood. As she sat on the sofa, she got a peek of the bedroom, the bed neatly made. This must be one of the weekly rentals, as it also boasted a small kitchen. Her gaze swept past the beer bottle on the counter. Had Grayson been drinking tonight?

As he took a seat next to her, the smell of tobacco wafted in her direction. She wrinkled her nose. One of her brothers smoked, and she couldn't stand it. One black mark against the perfect Grayson Rhodes.

"You're a smoker?"

His eyebrows shot up to single lock of blond hair on his forehead. "What? No, that was part of my disguise."

Remove the black mark. He *was* perfect.

"I'm sorry. Go ahead. What do you have?"

"I accepted an invitation to go out drinking with the crew after work at The Tavern. It's down by the pleasure boat side of the dock, near that diner."

She nodded. "I saw it."

"While I was there, two young women came into the bar, both with brown hair, about the same age as Chloe. I followed them into a back room with pool tables, and one of the dockworkers, nephew of my buddy, marched one of the girls out back."

"They didn't see you skulking around?"

"The Tavern is a hot spot, crowded, noisy. They didn't notice me. I couldn't follow them out the back exit, so I went out the front and circled around."

"You had cover?"

"Dumpster. Their voices carried in the alley. Bottom line—the nephew, a Tony Balducci, was threatening this girl Brandy to keep quiet. She was worried about the murders."

As Grayson recounted the conversation between Tony Balducci and Brandy, Aria's fingernails curled into the thin material covering the arm of the sofa. "'Blah boatie'? That's what he called them?"

"I figured 'blah' because they all look alike and 'boatie' because they must be doing something on a boat."

"Oh, my God. That makes me sick." She sat forward

on the edge of the sofa cushion. "He knew the baby was okay, but more importantly, he said the baby didn't get hurt because he was innocent. How would he come to that conclusion unless he was the killer?"

"My thoughts exactly."

"Grayson, this is huge. I suppose you didn't get a recording of them."

He reached for his phone on the table, his gray T-shirt stretching across his back muscles. "I didn't record the conversation—too far away and I didn't want any light or noises coming from my phone. But I took pictures of the women and I took a picture of Tony."

Scooting next to her, he held out his phone in front of her. "These are the two women. Brandy is the one on the right in the skirt."

"May I?" She covered his roughened hand with her own, moving the phone closer to her face. She studied the pretty girls. Both brunettes, the one on the left smiling and Brandy, on the right, wide-eyed with stiff posture. "She looks nervous."

"That's nothing compared to what she looked like after her meeting with Tony in the alley." Grayson swiped to the next picture. "Tony Balducci."

Grayson had caught Tony in profile, his dark hair swept back from a high forehead, long, dark lashes framing his eyes. She'd met hundreds of young, Italian men like Tony, working-class boys looking for a brighter future. Where had this one gone wrong?

"This is great. It's more than luck that led you to this discovery. You had an instinct about the docks, didn't you?"

"Just made sense."

"I'm sure I can make a case for bringing him in for questioning. You overheard a conversation that sounded suspicious." She rubbed her thumb across her chin. "But unless he confesses, I'm not sure we'll have anything to hold him. Not to say we can't keep an eye on him."

"There's more." Grayson put the phone in her lap as he bounded from the sofa. He gripped a beer bottle on the counter by the neck and lifted it. "I got Tony's DNA."

Aria's mouth dropped open. If Grayson ever got tired of making bundles of money, he could have a new career with the FBI. "How did you get that?"

"His uncle, Chuck O'Leary, is my buddy at work. We were all sitting together at the bar, so when Tony came back inside, he had a beer next to us. I just snagged the bottle when he left. Nobody noticed that it wasn't my beer. Like I said, lots of action in The Tavern."

"Do you have a bag for that bottle? We don't have any fingerprints from the crime scenes, but the fewer prints on that bottle, the better. I'm assuming we'll have the bartender's prints, yours."

"On the neck only. Tony had the bottle by the base." He ducked to slide open a drawer in the kitchen and popped up, waving a plastic grocery bag. "Will this work?"

"Perfect. Can you send these pictures to me, too?"

As Grayson carefully placed the bottle in the bag, he said, "You can do that. You're in my phone as AC."

She warranted a name in his phone?

Aria brought up his texts, found herself and attached

the pictures of Brandy and Tony. "Are you sure you weren't a detective in another life?"

"This is personal, Aria. When I heard that dirtbag threaten Brandy and slap her, I wanted to wring his neck with my bare hands. My sister made a lot of mistakes in her life, but she didn't deserve this ending. None of them did."

"The work you did tonight is going to go a long way to help solve your sister's murder." She drummed her fingers against his phone. "This doesn't end with Tony, though. He's just a grunt. We need to get to the top dog."

"I figured as much. That's why I didn't take down the little weasel where he stood." Grayson punched his fist into his palm, and all sorts of muscles rippled beneath his T-shirt.

Either his body had responded to the hard labor on the docks in spectacular fashion, or developing properties and making oodles of money was more strenuous than she'd imagined.

Her phone buzzed and she pulled it out to check that she'd received the text with the picture attachments. She pushed to her feet and sauntered into the kitchen, which could barely accommodate the two of them side by side.

"Thanks for turning this information over to me." She placed her phone on the counter next to the bagged bottle.

"Who else?" He shrugged.

"You could've given it to the PHPD or my director or supervisor, Rihanna. Thanks for trusting me with it."

He turned to face her, his blue eyes kindling. "You're

the only one I trust right now, Aria. You're the only one… I wanted to see."

His low voice vibrated, touching a chord deep within her. She swallowed and ran her tongue along her bottom lip. Bad move.

His gaze followed the sweep of her tongue and instead of sealing her lips like any professional FBI agent would do, she lodged the tip of her tongue in the corner of her mouth and met his eyes.

He tilted his head and brushed his knuckle across her cheek, a question in his eyes.

Her knees weakened along with her resolve, and she swayed toward him, pinching the material of his shirt between her fingertips. Was that a yes? She wanted it to be a yes.

His hand slid to the back of her head, cupping it in his palm, his fingers entangled in her hair.

Her lashes fluttered as she parted her lips, her heart thundering in her chest.

When he pressed his mouth against hers, it soothed an ache in her core she hadn't even realized she'd had until this moment. His tongue slid into her willing mouth, and she melted against him as he wound an arm around her waist to pull her closer to his body.

Their kiss deepened. Her arm encircled his neck. His pulse throbbed against the pads of her fingers as she skimmed them along the warm flesh of his throat.

Her phone buzzed on the countertop.

Grayson jerked away from her, leaving a blast of cold in his absence. "I'm so sorry. I…"

She dove for her phone, heat washing into her cheeks. In her confusion and haste, she didn't even check the display.

"Hello?"

Axel's voice, clipped and professional, greeted her. "Where are you? You're not in your room."

She stuttered some inanity and Axel cut her off. "Never mind. I'm not your daddy, but I thought you'd be interested in this piece of news, superstar."

Superstar? She felt anything but right now. She wiped her hand across her mouth, rubbing away Grayson's kiss.

"What news?"

"We got the rapid DNA van out here and you know that tissue you picked up at the Chloe Larsen murder site?"

"Yeah." Aria's gaze darted to Grayson, making a big deal out of washing a few dishes in the sink.

"It contains DNA."

"I figured it would. It's a tissue."

"Ah, let me finish." Axel paused for drama and a drumroll if he could have it. "We also collected DNA from beneath the fingernails of the third victim, and guess what?"

Aria sucked in a breath. "They're a match?"

"They are a match, which means we have the killer's DNA. Now we just have to find someone whose DNA is a match to the tissue and the skin, and we've got our guy."

Aria pressed her hand against her heart and grabbed

the back of Grayson's T-shirt. "I've got news for you, too, Axel. We found our guy and, with the DNA at the crime sites, we've got him dead to rights."

Chapter Nine

Aria touched her tender lower lip, still feeling Grayson's mouth against hers. She'd literally been saved by the bell…or the buzz. No telling how far she would've gone last night under that man's spell.

"Coffee." Max set a mug in front of her with a clunk. "You looked like you needed it."

"Thanks, Max." She picked up one of the little thimbles of creamer he'd dumped next to her cup. "Do I look that out of it?"

"You look like someone who's been working her tail off. Way to make a splash on this team." He put down his own cup and plopped into the chair next to hers at the table set up in their war room at the PD.

At least Max didn't think she looked like an agent who was mooning over a victim's brother. Let him think her exhaustion was all about the case—not that the murders hadn't robbed her of sleep, too.

Opaline had set up her computer at one end of the table and was clicking furiously on her keyboard with her long nails. She sighed. "Not exactly like home, but it'll do, and I wholly approve of the new scenery. I rate the Port Huron boys in blue a solid seven."

Max rolled his eyes. "Do these poor guys know they're being ranked and judged? There's a name for that when men do the same thing to women."

"It's called standard operating procedure." Opaline straightened the flowered clip in her hair, the ends blue this week.

Alana entered the room, closely followed by Amanda, and she took a seat next to Opaline. "Did you get all the pictures and graphics Amanda sent you?"

"Yes, ma'am. Created a slide show and everything." Opaline wiggled her fingers in the air. "Good morning, Carly, Rihanna, Axe."

Opaline's voice trailed off as her sister Selena followed Max into the room. Then she ducked her head and checked some cables going to the projector.

Aria took in the mask that had dropped over Selena's face. What was it with those two? Having four brothers, Aria would kill to have had a sister growing up.

Alana rapped on the table. "Axel, the door, please."

Axel tipped his chair back on its legs and reached across with his long arm to push the door closed.

"I'm sure you've all heard the exciting news by now." Alana folded her hands and practically beamed at them. "We have DNA from murders two and three, connecting those crimes—a discarded tissue from the Chloe Larsen scene and skin under the fingernails of the third victim."

Opaline brought up the first slide with a picture of the baggie containing the used tissue Aria had picked up at the second crime scene. Next to it was a close-up picture of the third victim's violet-polished nails, blood and tissue beneath them.

"Even more exciting, because this particular DNA is not in CODIS, we have a suspect along with the suspect's DNA. That suspect's DNA has been delivered to the rapid DNA van and we should have the results shortly. If the suspect's DNA matches that on the tissue and the skin from the fingernails, we have our guy."

Rihanna clapped and then looked around. "For being the media liaison, it seems I'm the only one out of the loop. Who is this guy and how'd we get a line on him?"

"Sorry, you were with CPS this morning, Rihanna, not that we want any of this getting out to the media yet." Alana touched Opaline's shoulder. "Show them what we have."

Tony Balducci's picture appeared on the screen, and Alana ID'd him. "This is Tony Balducci. He works at the docks, and he has no criminal record except for a few minor infractions as a juvenile. Someone working at the docks overheard him talking about the murders and threatening another young woman. We got his DNA from a beer bottle that he discarded."

"Sweet." Rihanna smoothed her thumb over her eyebrow. "Wait, isn't Chloe Larsen's brother, Grayson Rhodes, working undercover at the docks right now? Did we get this from him? Did you get this from him, Aria?"

"I did." Aria dropped her chin to her chest and relaxed all her muscles in the hopes that she could keep her blush at bay.

Alana came to her rescue. "Like I said, we're waiting on the DNA results to come back and then Max, Carly and Aria are going to bring him in. Do it without fanfare, but I'll let you decide how."

The next slide showed the two young women walking into The Tavern. Alana used her red penlight to circle Brandy's face. "This young woman may be in the same line of business as the other three. Her name is Brandy, and that's all we have. Max and Selena are going to track her down. Her friend's name is Rita, and we don't know whether or not she's involved. Find Rita, maybe you find Brandy."

Opaline clicked through more slides, showing the ballistics that matched the weapon for all three murders. She commented, "Max got the ballistics reports this morning and it confirmed the same gun was used in all three murders, a .22 caliber, small but deadly."

"I'm going to let Aria talk about motive. Our contact at the docks overheard some conversation between Balducci and Brandy, which led him to take that picture." Alana sat. "Take it away, Aria."

Aria stood and circled the table to take Alana's place next to Opaline. "When Balducci was talking to a very upset Brandy, he told her she had nothing to worry about if she followed the rules. He mentioned that the other women had gotten greedy and had to be dealt with."

Max whistled. "So, drug smugglers dipping into the product?"

"That's what it sounds like. Balducci also mentioned a name for the women."

Selena asked, "You mean Maddie Johnson—the name on the other vics' IDs?"

Aria braced her fingertips on the tabletop. "No. He called the women 'blah boaties.'"

Carly made a sound in the back of her throat and wrinkled her nose. "That makes me sick. Are you thinking what I'm thinking? 'Blah' because all the women looked alike? Nondescript brunettes with brown eyes?"

"And 'boaties' because they must be smuggling the drugs across the water." Max flattened his hands on the table, the whites of his nails standing out against his dark, brown skin, his two thumbs touching. "That hints at something big. This Balducci character is small-time. He's a cog in the wheel. We need to find the person spinning that wheel."

"When Axel and I are on the hunt for Brandy and Rita today, we'll check out the boat rentals at the pleasure dock. See if a Maddie Johnson has rented any boats recently."

Axel said, "While we're out there, if we have time, we'll take a boat to Canada ourselves. I think the most common trip from Port Huron is across the St. Clair River to Point Edward. Might be a good idea to see what's over there."

"Anything else, Aria?" Alana stood beside her.

"That's it."

"We all know what to do. Aria, Carly, Max, decide how you're going to bring in Balducci without making waves. Axel, Selena, find those young women so we don't have another victim on our hands." She tipped her head at the last slide, a picture of all three dead women. "Remember why we're doing this."

Chairs scraped and voices murmured as the meeting ended. Aria traipsed around to the other side of the table and pulled out the chair next to Rihanna. "Can I talk to you about something?"

"Absolutely. You're the hero of the hour." Rihanna pushed back from the table and crossed her legs, her knee-high boots squeaking as she swung one long leg over the other.

"Is there any way we can use rapid DNA for Danny and his uncle, Grayson Rhodes?" Aria held her breath.

Rihanna blinked her dark lashes. "We can't request it for a standard DNA test."

"If CPS can't ask for quicker results, can they just use what they have? Grayson showed you his pictures of him and his sister with Danny, right? He described the toys attached to Danny's car seat because he bought them for him. Isn't that enough to prove he's family?"

"I don't doubt he is, Aria, and neither does CPS, but there's protocol to follow." She tilted her head, wrapping one of her curls around her finger. "He really got to you, didn't he?"

Rihanna had no idea.

"It's just that I want to do something for him after he did all this for us. He brought us Tony Balducci. Even with Balducci's DNA from the crime scenes, we wouldn't have been able to ID him because he wasn't in the Combined DNA Index System. We'd still be flailing around if Grayson hadn't stalked Balducci at the bar and eavesdropped on his conversation—at great danger to himself, I might add." Aria flushed as her final words rang out, louder than she'd planned, turning a few heads.

"I'll tell you what." Rihanna patted Aria's hand. "I'll talk to CPS and see if Grayson can visit Danny with the foster family. The evidence he showed us is compelling enough that we all believe he's Danny's uncle. Danny even has those same impossibly blue eyes…but then, you probably know all about those eyes, don't you?"

Aria's mouth gaped open until Rihanna cracked a smile and said, "I don't blame you, sister."

"Thanks, Rihanna."

Max pounded his fist on the table. "Everyone out, except Carly, Aria and me. We got a bad guy to take down."

Aria scooted closer to the table, folding her hands to make up for her previous outburst. She shouldn't be getting so personally involved in her first case, should she? But Grayson deserved a break.

"I verified Balducci's working today. We can pick him up at lunch, but we don't want to alarm his co-workers—just in case any of them are involved. Carly, you approach him first." Max held up his hands. "Sorry, ladies, Balducci is the type of guy who's not going to expect a female cop coming at him. He'll probably feel more comfortable with one of you."

"A lot of the guys bring their lunches and eat at some tables on the dock when it's not raining or snowing. Even Carly can't go marching in there without arousing some suspicion." Aria tapped on her laptop as she entered notes. "There is a lunch truck that comes in, but there's no guarantee Balducci will get his lunch there."

"We have to make sure he does. You have a connection at the docks—use him." Max raised his brows at Aria.

"I—I could ask Grayson if he can get Balducci out to the food truck." Aria sucked in her bottom lip. Were they exploiting Grayson's hunger to nail Chloe's killer?

Carly tucked a strand of blond hair behind her ear. "That would work. I can approach him there and tell him we have a few questions, get him away from the truck, and go in for the arrest."

"I hope his DNA comes back as a match, because we can't hold him based on an overheard conversation and, once he's out—" Max flicked his fingers "—he'll be gone like a cool breeze off the lake."

They discussed their plan for another thirty minutes and then Max leveled a finger at Aria. "Can you make that call now?"

"Grayson really does work when he's there, so it's better if I text him." Aria pulled out her phone and sent a text to Grayson asking him to try to get Tony out to the food truck at lunch. She had faith he could get the job done.

Carly rose first. "I think it's a good idea if we stick around the station. I'm going to get something to drink and work on those drug reports. Anyone want anything?"

Max held up his phone. "My ex-wife's been trying to reach me about our son. I'm going to step out and call her."

"I'm fine, Carly. I'm going to nurse this lukewarm coffee Max brought me earlier and do some work in here, if nobody minds."

"I think it's ours for the time being." Carly held the door open for Max, and they both slipped out of the war room.

Aria continued with her notes, taking surreptitious glances at her phone. She and Grayson hadn't spoken much after that kiss last night.

After Axel's call, she'd told Grayson about the DNA matches at the crime scenes, but they'd avoided the elephant in the room...and had avoided any additional contact with each other. He'd acted as if she'd had a repellent bubble around her, keeping him a good five feet out of her aura—and that's the only way she could've operated around him.

He'd apologized again when he'd walked her out to her car in the seedy motel's parking lot, as if he'd pounced on her in a moment of weakness when she'd been a willing participant the whole way.

Something Max had said stuck in her throat. He'd called Grayson a contact and had advised Aria to use him. Would Grayson feel that way when he received her text asking for his help? Would he think that's why she'd allowed the kiss last night?

Carly had pulled out the chair across from Aria before she even realized she'd returned to the room. "You snuck in here like a cat."

"No, I didn't. You were just concentrating so hard on your work, you didn't hear me." Carly planted one elbow on the table and cupped her chin with the palm. "You know, I have to tell you, we're all really impressed with you. You're a great asset and you fit in like you've been on the team for years. Alana is so good at spotting people and recognizing just who we need."

"Thanks. I have to admit you all intimidated me that first day. All so accomplished." Aria picked up her phone. "Text from Grayson Rhodes."

He'd texted just three little words. Count on me.

She didn't need any more than that from him. She knew she could.

"Good news?" Carly peered at her over the rim of her soda can. "That smile makes you look like the cat who swallowed the canary, or the cream, or whatever."

Aria tapped her phone and folded her arms. What had happened to her poker face, the one she'd used to lure dozens of drug dealers into a false sense of security? She'd become an open book—a silly, smitten, open book.

"Grayson indicated he'd take care of getting Balducci out to the lunch truck. I'm not going to ask how, but after his feats last night at that bar, I'm not worried."

"Attractive guy, isn't he?" Carly ran her fingertip around the rim of her can. "Rich, angsty."

"Angsty?" A laugh bubbled to Aria's lips despite her best effort. "Whatever that means."

"Oh, come on. He lost his sister, he's trying to reclaim his nephew, he's bound and determined to see justice done."

"Are you telling me I'm getting sucked into an image?"

"I'm telling you to be careful. This job—" she circled her finger in the air to encompass the room with the bulletin board of pictures and lines of string connecting those pictures, Opaline's laptop with the gruesome slideshow of murder victims and their crime scenes, the discarded coffee cups and empty bags of potato chips "—doesn't lend itself well to a personal life, marriage, kids."

Aria scooped in a deep breath, ready to protest that marriage with Grayson Rhodes had never occurred to her. Max's entrance and his fist pump saved her from protesting too much.

"We got him. The DNA from the beer bottle matches the DNA from the tissue and the skin beneath Jane Doe number three's fingernails. It's enough to arrest, charge and hold him."

Carly met Aria's eyes and, with a lilt to her voice, said, "Perfect. Aria's guy is going to get Balducci out to the truck. We're golden."

Max rolled his wrist inward and checked his watch. "We have just about an hour until go time. Anyone need to change clothes, pick up a different weapon, stash their stuff back at the hotel? I'm going to grab a sandwich at that place across the street from the hotel."

"I'd like to drop off my bag." Aria snapped her laptop closed. "And maybe we should clean up this room, so the cops don't think we're all a bunch of slobs."

"Way ahead of you." Max dangled a plastic garbage bag from his fingers. "Alana and Amanda are coming back in a few, so they can start messing it up again."

Carly picked up a half-full chip bag and swung it back and forth. "I don't think it's Alana and Amanda we have to worry about."

They spent a few minutes picking up, locked the

room behind them and piled into Carly's rental for the ride back to the hotel. Max peeled off to get his sandwich, and Aria and Carly ducked into their rooms.

Aria put her bag with the laptop on the desk and downed the rest of the water left in the bottle by the nightstand. Standing in front of the full-length mirror, she secured her holstered SIG-Sauer and yanked her sweater over it.

This morning she didn't know she'd be in on the arrest, but she'd dressed more casually in jeans and low-heeled boots, as the other team members seemed to dress down away from the office in Traverse City. Tipping her foot onto her toe, she studied the heel of her boot. Could she run in these if she had to?

The crepe-soled shoes she wore on patrol gave her fleet feet, but running shoes would be even better and she could actually get away with wearing them with jeans. She sat on the edge of the bed and traded her boots for a pair of sneakers. Then she grabbed her jacket and went downstairs to meet the others.

When Max saw her from the lobby, he stuffed the rest of his sandwich in his mouth and brushed his hands over the yellow paper on the table in front of him. "Carly's waiting for us out front in the car. You ready?"

"I used to work patrol, remember? This stuff is second nature to me."

"I know. My buddy took a job with the LAPD when we got back from deployment. He said working patrol on the streets of L.A. was more dangerous than being in Iraq."

"Detroit's no picnic, either." She gave Max a wide berth as he pushed up from the soft lobby sofa.

"Relax. I'm not going to fall over on you." He cracked a smile and tapped his leg below the knee. "Like you said, second nature."

Aria put a hand to her throat. "I'm sorry. Is that how I looked?"

"Don't worry about it. It's the typical reaction when people first find out about my leg, but they get used to it."

"If I hadn't read your bio, I don't think I would've even realized you had a prosthetic."

"That's due to the ingenious stuff the engineers keep coming up with." He stepped aside and allowed her to exit the automatic doors ahead of him.

As they reached the car, Max bent his head toward the driver's-side window. "Remember? You're letting Aria drive. That way we have a driver behind the wheel in case we need to take off while you're talking to the suspect."

"Oops, forgot already." Carly slid out of the car and jogged around the back, while Aria took her place.

She moved the seat up a bit and waited until both Max and Carly were in place before taking off. As planned, she dropped off Max a block from the docks and left Carly next to the food truck. She parked farther down the street with a view of the docks and the truck.

As the digital clock in the car ticked over to twelve o'clock, the activity at the docks seemed to shift away from the boats and the water and surge toward the office buildings up front and the parking lot.

Although Carly had seen the picture of Tony, when Aria spotted him swaggering through the parking lot, she shot Carly a quick text that he was on his way. She knew she could count on Grayson.

Max had moved within striking distance of the food truck, and Aria swallowed as the players moved into position like pieces on a chessboard—with Tony Balducci as the pawn. But who was the king?

Looking both ways, Tony jogged across the street. When he reached the lunch truck, he shoved his hands into his pockets and studied the menu board out front.

Carly made her move. She pivoted toward Tony and began talking to him. Tony's posture changed. The hands came out of the pockets and his spine straightened.

As Carly reached into her pocket for her badge and ID, Tony's head twisted to one side and then the other. Aria clutched the door handle. She recognized the signs of a runner, and Tony was displaying Usain Bolt level ones.

His legs bicycled backward a few steps and then he pivoted and took off—right toward Max. Max was ready. As Tony ran past him, Max's arm shot out and he grabbed him, slowing his pace.

Tony twisted away from him and ran into the street, toward the boats, with both Max and Carly on his tail.

Aria jumped from the car and joined the chase, her sneakers giving her lightning speed. Tony's work boots slowed him as they pounded against the metal decking of the marina dock. Aria reached him as he turned onto a gangway of a boat bobbing in its slip.

She grabbed the back of his jacket but couldn't hold him. Then Max came out of nowhere and tackled Tony to the ground.

"I didn't do nothing. I didn't do nothing." Tony squirmed beneath Max's knee planted firmly on his back.

When Max slapped on the cuffs, Tony slackened like a rag doll. Max hauled him to his feet.

"Why'd you run if you didn't do anything?" Carly wedged a hand on her side, panting. "We just want to talk to you."

Her own breath heaving, Aria said, "That's right, Tony. We just want to talk to you about the dead blah boaties."

"4 for 4" MINI-SURVEY

We are prepared to **REWARD** you with 4 FREE Books and Free Gifts for completing our MINI SURVEY!

Suspenseful Romance

Suspense

You'll get up to...

4 FREE BOOKS & FREE GIFTS

FREE Value Over $20!

just for participating in our Mini Survey!

Get Up To 4 Free Books!

Dear Reader,

IT'S A FACT: if you answer 4 quick questions, we'll send you 4 FREE REWARDS from each series you try!

Try **Harlequin® Romantic Suspense** books featuring heart-racing page-turners with unexpected plot twists and irresistible chemistry that will keep you guessing to the very end.

Try **Harlequin Intrigue® Larger-Print** books featuring action-packed stories that will keep you on the edge of your seat. Solve the crime and deliver justice at all costs.

Or **TRY BOTH!**

I'm not kidding you. As a leading publisher of women's fiction, we value your opinions... and your time. That's why we are prepared to reward you handsomely for completing our mini-survey. In fact, we have 4 Free Rewards for you, including 2 free books and 2 free gifts from each series you try!

Thank you for participating in our survey,

Pam Powers

To get your 4 FREE REWARDS:
Complete the survey below and return the insert today to receive up to 4 FREE BOOKS and FREE GIFTS guaranteed!

"4 for 4" MINI-SURVEY

1 Is reading one of your favorite hobbies?
☐ YES ☐ NO

2 Do you prefer to read instead of watch TV?
☐ YES ☐ NO

3 Do you read newspapers and magazines?
☐ YES ☐ NO

4 Do you enjoy trying new book series with FREE BOOKS?
☐ YES ☐ NO

Please send me my Free Rewards, consisting of **2 Free Books from each series I select** and **Free Mystery Gifts**. I understand that I am under no obligation to buy anything, as explained on the back of this card.

☐ **Harlequin® Romantic Suspense** (240/340 HDL GQ5A)
☐ **Harlequin Intrigue® Larger-Print** (199/399 HDL GQ5A)
☐ **Try Both** (240/340 & 199/399 HDL GQ5M)

FIRST NAME _____ LAST NAME _____

ADDRESS _____

APT.# _____ CITY _____

STATE/PROV. _____ ZIP/POSTAL CODE _____

EMAIL ☐ Please check this box if you would like to receive newsletters and promotional emails from Harlequin Enterprises ULC and its affiliates. You can unsubscribe anytime.

HI/HRS-520-MS20

Chapter Ten

Tony cooled his heels at the Port Huron jail while Amanda ran down Axel. Alana wanted him to lead the interrogation of Tony, and she wanted Aria to sit in and watch the master.

Tony had clammed up on them on the drive over, but they'd expected that. He didn't know what they had on him, but once they told him, he might rethink his silence. If he called his uncle and got himself an attorney, they could be facing a longer process, but they had his DNA at both scenes. Science didn't lie.

Alana had contacted the shift supervisor at the docks and told him they had Tony Balducci in custody but wanted to keep it quiet. The supervisor agreed and when Aria had sent Grayson a quick text, he'd confirmed that not even Tony's uncle was aware of what had gone down.

Most of the team converged in the war room to wait for Axel.

Amanda held up her phone. "That was Selena. They're on their way. They didn't have any luck finding Brandy, but they might have a line on her friend, Rita."

Alana praised the arrest team. "Good job bringing him in. Max, you okay after that tackle?"

He gave them a thumbs-up while he dug into another sandwich from the order Amanda had placed for the team.

"Rihanna is preparing a press release, letting the media know we have an arrest in the cases, but she's not going live with it yet. We don't want to scare anyone off—or put anyone in danger."

Aria pointed to a sandwich near Carly and then pointed to herself. "Is that turkey?"

"Yep." Carly shot the sandwich across the smooth table, and Aria snagged it before it launched onto the floor. "Chips?"

"Barbecue."

Alana removed her glasses. "I'm sorry. Am I interrupting your lunch?"

"Actually, you are." Carly popped a chip in her mouth.

"Okay, eat. We'll wait for Axel, and then I want to review with him what we want out of Balducci—and Axel will get it, eventually."

As they were eating, Amanda answered her phone. When she hung up, she said, "Axel wants the cops to move Tony Balducci into the interrogation room now. He said, give him time to stew."

Alana looked up from her computer. "Max, could you go down and make sure they bring him over from his cell to the interrogation room?"

A few minutes later, Max returned. "That's taken care of. Small room, no windows, stationary chair for him—just the way we like it."

Another thirty minutes passed before Axel arrived. "I wanted to give Tony some time alone, so I dropped Selena off at the hotel. She's training with Blanca." He rubbed his hands together. "Are you ready, Aria?"

"I am." She balled up her sandwich paper and chip bag and tossed them into the wastebasket. "Anything for Tony?"

"We'll give him his choice from the vending machines. He's our guest here—for a little while." Axel ran a hand through his messy blond hair.

In fact, Aria had never seen Axel so...casual before. His jeans, basic Wrangler, were faded at the knees and he wore his waffle-print Henley untucked and rolled up at the sleeves. He looked ready to meet Tony on an even playing field.

As they took the stairs down to the interrogation room, Axel cocked his head toward hers. "Feel free to chime in at any time with questions of your own, and don't be surprised if I bring you into the conversation with Tony. He's been isolated long enough, and we're going to go right in and build rapport with him. We don't want him to ask for an attorney. We don't want him to know what we have on him right away. Let's make him comfortable."

Axel's steady stream of instructions ended when they reached the interrogation room at the end of the hall.

As she followed Axel into the room, Aria glanced at the claustrophobic four walls. Max hadn't been kidding about the size.

Tony glanced up from his seat in the corner, a table to

his right and two chairs across from him, his ankle resting on his alternate knee, his foot jiggling up and down.

"Hey, Tony." Axel turned on the megawatt smile and thrust out his hand. "I'm Supervisory Agent Axel Morrow, and this is Special Agent Aria Calletti. Are you comfortable?"

Axel didn't wait for an answer because, of course, Tony wasn't comfortable in that hard metal chair. "Do you want something to drink? Coffee? Soda? Wish we could offer you a beer, but that's not on the menu."

Tony swallowed and he gripped the edge of the table. "Yeah, a Coke, please."

"Aria?"

"Sure, I'll be right back with that. Anything else? Chips? Cookies?"

Tony's gaze bounced from her face to Axel's as if he couldn't believe his good fortune. "Yeah, chips *and* cookies. I never got my lunch."

A little bit of belligerence was okay. Showed he thought he was in control.

"I'll be right back." She snapped the door behind her and jogged down the hallway to the vending machines. She pulled some bills out of her pocket and fed them in the slot with shaky fingers. She didn't want to miss anything.

Hugging the chips and cookies to her chest and clutching the soda in her hand, she scurried back to the room. She tapped on the door once and Axel invited her in.

"Here you go." She dumped the bags in front of Tony

and placed the can next to the snacks. "Hope those are okay."

"I was just asking Tony how he liked working on the docks, and you know what he told me?"

"What?" Aria took her seat and gave Tony an encouraging smile.

"It's just a temporary gig for him. He wants to be a rapper."

Aria widened her eyes. "Really? There's a guy from my hometown who just cut his first demo."

They let Tony ramble on about his nonexistent rap career for a few minutes and then Axel smacked the table, making both Aria and Tony jump.

"Hey, you know Aria here is from an Italian family, too. Maybe you know some of the same people."

Aria laughed and met Tony's eyes, which had lost some of the deer-in-the-headlights look. "Agent Morrow thinks all Italian families in Michigan know each other."

Tony gave a nervous titter like a schoolgirl trying to fit in with the cool kids but not understanding their jokes.

Axel continued to use his charm to disarm Tony, who'd started to explain to Axel who the Lions needed in their next draft.

They talked for a good long time and, as every minute passed, it was clear Tony moved from wary to relaxed to nervous again. Axel was wearing him down with the mere passage of time, and the skillful agent seemed to have the instincts to tell when the precise moment was to strike to get what they needed.

With a smile still on his handsome face, Axel asked, "Who's using drugs in Port Huron, Tony?"

Tony blinked and his Adam's apple bobbed. "N-nobody. I don't use no drugs."

Axel spread his hands. "Oh, we know *you* don't use drugs, but there's a drug culture here for sure. Lotta chicks use? Put out for a little weed?"

Aria's stomach churned, but she kept her face impassive.

Tony's bottom lip jutted forward. "Yeah, there are a few of those girls around."

"Brandy one of those? Maddie? Rita?"

A red stain stood out on Tony's neck. "I dunno. I don't know them girls."

Lie number one.

"You don't?" Axel's brows shot up. "Those girls are involved in the drug trade. Maybe they got what they deserved, maybe not."

Tony nodded and then stopped himself, covering his mouth with his hand.

"How do you think those drugs are getting across to Canada, Tony?"

"Smuggling drugs to Canada? I don't know nothing about that."

"When was the last time you were in Canada? Right across the river, you must go there a lot."

"I—" Tony rolled his eyes upward, searching for his answer on the ceiling "—not sure. I don't remember. I didn't…"

"Sure, you did." Axel cut off Tony with a slicing motion of his hand.

Tony's gaze slid to Aria, confusion wrinkling his brow. "I was gonna say I didn't have nothing to do with the murder of those girls."

"I know what you were going to say." Axel patted the file folder. "C'mon, Tony. We know you did *that*. We're just trying to figure out if you're the guy in charge."

Tony's wild eyes skimmed across the bulging folder on the table and then flew to Aria's face. "Is he kidding?"

"Oh, I don't know. You seem like a bright guy. It's not so far-fetched that you're the kingpin of this operation." Aria folded her hands in her lap.

"Kingpin? I ain't no kingpin. What the hell?"

"But you know who is." Axel leaned back in his chair, crossing his hands behind his head.

"I don't know who the kingpin is. I just do what I'm told."

Aria sipped in a small breath. If Tony realized he'd just admitted to there being a smuggling ring in Port Huron and that he worked in that ring, he didn't seem to realize it.

She hunched forward, elbows on her knees. "You did a good thing, Tony. You spared that little baby. That tells us something about your character."

Tony slumped. His chin dropped to his chest and his shoulders rolled forward. The classic posture of surrender.

"I—I couldn't hurt the baby. They didn't tell me nothing about a baby."

A muscle at the side of Axel's mouth jumped. "You even reported the baby to 9-1-1, so he wouldn't have to stay out there by himself all night. We knew we were dealing with someone…special, someone with a conscience."

"I couldn't just leave the baby there. My sister has a kid. My niece is around the same age as that baby. No way was I gonna leave that baby there. He wasn't gonna be no witness, anyway." He lifted his chin. "Is he all right?"

Aria answered. "The baby is fine—thanks to you."

Of course, he has no mother, thanks to you.

"How'd you find me?"

"DNA." Axel shook his head. "Almost nobody gets away with murder these days, Tony. Your bosses should've told you that, too. They don't care about you. They didn't even tell you one of your targets was going to have a baby with her, did they?"

Tony's dark eyes got darker, and a mulish look played about his mouth. "Nobody told me nothing about that baby."

"That's right." Axel's voice soothed, dripped with understanding. "Those are some bad people who don't have your best interests at heart. They're not like family, Tony."

"No, they're not." Tony thumped his chest with his fist. "Family is everything."

"Who are they? Give me some names." Axel whipped out a sheet of paper and held a pen, poised at the top, as if he expected all the names right now.

Tony's mouth formed a stubborn line. "I got nothing for you, man. I don't know the names. I follow orders."

"All right." Axel rotated the piece of paper 180 degrees with the tip of his finger so that it faced Tony. "We need you to write down everything you know, everything about those three murders you committed."

Tony licked his lips and wiped the back of his grimy hand across his nose, leaving a streak of dirt on his face.

"And the baby you saved." Aria leaned forward and put a hand on his arm.

His arm twitched beneath her touch, but he picked up the pen and started writing. He talked as he wrote, filling in more details about the killings, including the third victim and how she'd lunged at him before he got off his shot, scratching the side of his neck.

As he pulled down the collar of his jacket to show them the scratch, still red, the knots in Aria's gut tightened.

He continued to write, and Aria asked, "Who's this Maddie Johnson? Is she a real person?"

His pen stopped moving, drilling an inky hole in the paper. "Nah, that's just the fake name they came up with. They gave all the girls the Maddie Johnson ID, made them dye their hair the same color brown and even wear contact lenses if they didn't have brown eyes."

An image of Grayson's blue eyes flashed across her mind. Chloe's must've been the same color.

"Why?" Axel asked. "Why the same look for them all?"

"IDs. Like I said. We had the Maddie Johnson ID for women who looked like that."

Axel flipped open the file and shuffled some papers. "How'd they get into Canada with the drugs?"

Aria held her breath. Tony hadn't actually admitted

to knowing about the smuggling scheme yet, but he'd just admitted to killing three women and he seemed in a loquacious mood.

"Oh, they had Maddie Johnson passports, too." Tony waved his hand in the air. "They all used the same boat, a motorboat for a pleasure cruise across the river. Some pleasure cruise—it was loaded up with Dance Fever and Blues."

Axel interjected. "Blues?"

Aria supplied the answer. "Oxy."

"Go on." Axel crossed his arms. "Where'd the Maddie Johnsons get the drugs?"

"Tunnels by the docks, man. I think they're stored there, and the blah boaties pick 'em up and ferry 'em across the river. The sellers are on the pleasure cruise with the drugs."

Axel peppered Tony with more questions before he could have time to pause and think. "Pleasure cruise goes into Point Edward in Canada? How do they get the drugs in? Are there more tunnels on the other side?"

Tony tugged on his earlobe. "Yeah, Point Edward. I don't know how they hide the drugs, and I don't know about no other tunnels. Just the ones on this side."

"Where are those tunnels?" To stop her hands from fidgeting on the table, Aria shoved them beneath her thighs. They were getting more info out of Tony than she'd ever expected…but they needed the top dog.

"I don't know that, either." Tony shook his head back and forth. "I'm gonna keep writing. I can't talk and write at the same time."

When Tony finished scribbling out his confession,

Axel cocked his head. "You sure you don't want to tell us who gave you the orders?"

Tony dropped the pen and held up his hands, a little drop of blue ink staining his thumb. "I don't know. Like I wrote in here, someone left me the burner phone and the .22. Hey, do you think I can get a special deal for helping that baby?"

Axel screwed up his mouth. "Maybe, but if you could give us those names of the people at the top, that might go down easier."

Tony's jaw hardened. "I dunno."

After almost three hours, Tony was clearly done and they'd gotten his confession for the murders, so at least other young women would be safe.

Axel wrapped up the interview with Tony, promising him they'd visit again, and then they left him in the in-terrogation room for the cops to return him to his cell.

When they got clear of the interrogation room, Axel gave her a fist bump. "Good work in there, Aria."

"Tony really thought we were his best friends—until we weren't."

"He still thinks we're his best friends, and we're going to keep it that way until we get the name of the person running the show."

"Do you think he knows?" She placed one foot on the first step of the staircase leading to the war room and turned toward Axel.

"Oh, he knows. He's afraid to tell us. He wants to make sure he doesn't get whacked in prison. But he'll figure out soon enough that, even if he keeps his mouth shut, he has a lot to worry about inside, especially without our protection." He shrugged. "He'll come around."

"We'll have to play up the fact that he didn't kill little Danny, and we know he's not all bad."

"Yeah, we'll play that up." Axel stepped past her and jogged up the steps, calling over his shoulder, "But he's still a killer."

Chapter Eleven

Grayson didn't want to raise any alarms, so after work he met the boys for a few beers at The Tavern. Nobody seemed to know what had happened to Tony Balducci, not even his uncle Chuck, and Grayson wanted to keep it that way.

The FBI must've contacted the supervisor, Bud Ellison, because Bud told someone Tony had left for the day feeling sick.

Grayson had gotten a text from Aria that Tony had confessed to the murders, but nothing else. He'd kept his lips zipped on the mastermind.

He'd waited for another text from her, but she'd gone radio silent—probably regretted that kiss. Probably didn't want to see him again. Why would she? She figured his part in this drama was over. But she didn't know him...yet. He wouldn't give up until the person responsible for Chloe's murder was behind bars—or dead.

When he and his coworkers bellied up to the bar, Grayson bought the first round and then took his beer to the back room to play some pool. One game, be visible, and then he had to get out of there.

Will got a table first and invited Grayson to play with him. As Grayson chalked up his stick, he caught sight of Rita, giggling on the arm of some buffed-up dude.

Grayson moved around the table, taking shots, bantering with Will and a few women looking on. Out of the corner of his eye, he noticed Rita edging closer and closer to the pool table, her beefy friend nowhere to be seen.

When Will stopped to talk strategy with one of the young women who'd been dogging him, Rita touched Grayson's elbow and, through her smile, whispered, "That girl I was with last night—Brandy? She wants to meet with you later."

Grayson grinned and nodded. Pointing to an angle on the table, he answered, "Why me?"

"I don't know. She said you were nice. She's in trouble."

He hoped nobody else in the bar had noticed his concern for the frightened woman. He rapped his knuckles on the edge of the table. "C'mon, Will. The shot's not going to get any easier unless you let Becca take it for you."

As Will guffawed and bent over Becca, his arms wrapped around her in the guise of helping her with the cue, Grayson took a step closer to Rita. "Why not call the cops?"

"She's scared. Look, I don't know what she's mixed up in, but she's in real trouble here. Can you meet her or not?"

Grayson kept his voice low. "Yeah, yeah. I'll meet her. Where and when?"

Rita stuck two fingers in the back pocket of his jeans and whistled. "Atta girl, Becca." Then she spun around and met the pumped-up dude as he returned with her glass of wine.

Grayson blew out a long breath. He had no intention of meeting Brandy on his own. The FBI would want to talk to this woman. She must've heard somehow that Tony was off the streets.

Grayson finished the game with Will, intentionally losing to speed things up, and said his goodbyes to his coworkers. He sauntered outside and dove into his back pocket for the slip of paper Rita had put there.

She'd written "9:00 p.m. on the *Fun Times*, slip 128." Grayson glanced toward the marina, the colored lights on display for Christmas, and wondered where slip 128 was located. Was she there now? She must be scared to reach out to a stranger.

He hesitated for two seconds before pulling out his phone and calling Aria. He had a perfectly legitimate reason for calling her, but he still let out a sigh when she picked up after two rings.

"Grayson?"

He got straight to the point, so she wouldn't miscon-strue his call as anything other than business. "Brandy contacted me through her friend Rita and wants to meet me in less than an hour at the marina."

"You're kidding. We've had two agents looking for Rita and Brandy all morning. Why you?"

"I guess Brandy trusts me because I asked after her last night, probably a stupid thing to do, drawing attention to myself, but I thought about Chloe when I saw her after Tony threatened her, and I couldn't stop myself."

"No, that looks like a good move on your part. I wonder why she doesn't call the cops."

"Scared."

"Are you supposed to come alone and all that?"

"The note I got didn't say, but I figured Brandy wouldn't be spooked to see me with a woman—might even make her feel better, but I think just you. We don't want to scare her off."

"No, of course not. I do have to give my director a heads-up, but it's important for us to talk to Brandy. She might be able to tell us something about the tunnels."

"Tunnels?"

"Some info we got from Tony. I'll tell you later. I have some other news for you…good news."

"About Danny?" Grayson gripped the phone so hard, it dug into his palm.

"Rihanna talked to the foster family, and they're willing to let you visit Danny. Even though the DNA isn't back yet, they saw your pictures and know that you accurately described his car seat."

A rush of emotion made him unable to speak for a few seconds and then he managed to strangle out a few words. "That's great. Thanks, Aria."

"It was all Rihanna." She cleared her throat. "Where do you want me to meet you?"

"Behind the boat rental shack. I'm outside The Tavern right now, and it's quiet along the marina."

"I'll be there in about thirty minutes." She ended

the call and he stood tapping the edge of the phone against his chin.

Even though she'd minimized her role, Aria had gone to bat for him with Rihanna and CPS. His getting to see Danny wouldn't have an impact on the case, wouldn't benefit Aria in any way. She'd helped him out because she had a big heart.

With time to kill, Grayson wandered toward the diner, turning up his collar against the wind. He scanned the interior through the windows first, to make sure nobody from the docks was there. They were more likely to be at The Tavern. But there were plenty of family men on the job who might be eating out.

He didn't recognize a soul, so he ducked inside and stationed himself at the counter. He ordered a piece of warm apple pie and a coffee.

He'd let Aria do the talking when they met with Brandy. She'd obviously gotten a lot of information from Tony Balducci today and had a better understanding of what they were dealing with now. Brandy just might be able to steer them to the person calling the shots.

He finished his pie and ordered two coffees to go. As the waitress behind the counter reached for the second to-go cup, Grayson, said, "Wait. Can you make that second cup a hot tea?"

"Sure, hon. What kind of tea?" She rattled off a bunch of catchy names until he held up his hands.

"Maybe one of those herb teas you mentioned. You pick."

She filled up the cup with hot water and then dredged a tea bag in it before capping it.

With a cup in each hand, Grayson pushed open the door with his foot. The cold hit his face like an icy rag and his eyes watered. He arched his shoulders and made his way to the boat rental office, decked out in holiday cheer, a red-nosed Santa in the window. He slipped behind the office, leaning his back against the faded wood, and placing one cup on the window ledge.

On the edge of the darkness, beyond the lights of the parking lot, a lone figure zigzagged between the cars. He could tell from her quick, light gait that it was Aria, although she kept to the shadows.

He squinted into the night, making sure nobody was following or watching her. His brain understood she was a special agent with the FBI and she was packing heat, but his instinct reacted to a petite woman, walking on her own in a deserted area at night. He couldn't turn off that part of him, so he watched her with eagle eyes, his muscles coiled, his hand hovering over the weapon he had in his jacket pocket.

The black beanie on her head, pulled over her loose hair, and her flushed cheeks somehow made her look even more defenseless. He knew better than to remark on this or to coddle her. Aria took her professionalism very seriously…and he did, too.

When she reached him, she smacked her gloved hands together. "It's chilly out here, and it's not even December."

"I hope that means a white Christmas—Danny's first." He handed her the cup with the paper end of the tea bag fluttering in the breeze. "I got you some tea. You mentioned you didn't like to drink coffee late."

Her dark eyes widened as she took the cup from him. "Thank you."

"It's herb tea. I have some packets of sugar in my pocket if you drink it like that."

"Plain is fine." She popped the lid and walked to the trash can at the corner of the building. She plucked up the string on the tea bag, held the dripping bag over her cup for a few seconds then tossed the bag into the garbage.

She pivoted and returned to his side. "Rita gave you a note?"

He pulled it from his pocket and shook it out for her. "Short and sweet."

Leaning in, she read the note. "I wonder what she thinks she's going to get from you. Protection?"

"We'll find out in about ten minutes." He wedged a shoulder against the wooden structure. "Tell me about Tony."

"He confessed to the murders." Aria reached out and touched the hand he'd bunched into a fist at his side. "I'm sorry. He confessed to all three. They were hits. He was ordered to take out those women."

"Why?" He'd known Tony was the killer, had barely been able to look the guy in the face this morning at work, but the news still hit him like a sledgehammer to the chest.

"The women, including your sister, had been hired to run drugs across the river to Canada, and they started skimming." She blew the steam from her tea and took a sip. "It's an old story, Grayson. As long as there have been drug dealers and drug runners, there has been skimming, stealing, sampling, you name it—and it usually doesn't end well for the skimmers."

"Dammit. Why would Chloe play with fire like that? She knew she could ask me for money at any time." He squeezed his eyes closed and tossed his coffee onto the ground with a splash. "Who am I kidding? As long as she was using, I wouldn't give her money."

"Why would you? Give her money to kill herself? She took a chance, just like the other women. Even if they hadn't been double-crossing the boss, they were living a precarious existence. We don't even know if Tony is telling the truth or if he knew the truth. Maybe the kingpin just wanted to get rid of these particular dealers. We don't know enough yet, Grayson."

"Do you think he'll tell you who's in charge?"

"The other agent I'm working with is a great interrogator, so I'm sure he'll get it out of him. If not?" As they passed the trashcan, she dropped her cup inside, and he followed with his empty cup. "Maybe Brandy will tell us."

They walked to the boats together, their shoulders bumping occasionally, Grayson's instincts on high alert. When he'd been here on his own, he hadn't sensed the same level of danger that now pricked the back of his neck, giving him the urge to grab on to Aria's hand and keep her safe.

The circumstances and the scene, the masts of the boats jutting into the sky, the ballasts creaking and whining, were shifting his imagination into overdrive.

If anything, Aria could not only look after herself, she could probably protect him, too.

But he'd failed to guard one woman from evil, he had no intention of falling short again.

Aria brushed her fingers against his hand. "Slips 110 to 130 up ahead. We should find *Fun Times* at the end of this row. I—I mean, *Fun Times*, the boat."

"Got it." He entwined his fingers with hers. "Somehow I don't think there are fun times ahead."

She nodded at a big powerboat sporting colored lights, an American and a French flag flapping in the breeze. "That's a nice one."

"Beautiful Place."

"Port Huron? It's nice, but I wouldn't call it beautiful."

He pointed back at the big boat they'd just passed. "The name of the boat—*Beautiful Place*."

"Oh, I guess that would be their beautiful place."

He kept hold of her hand until they reached slip 128, and then she disentangled her fingers from his.

His boots made more noise on the metal walkway than her sneakers, so he tried to lighten his step. When they drew closer to the boat, a twenty-five-foot bow rider, its outer railings decorated with Christmas lights, Grayson peered at the deck. "Brandy?"

When silence met his tentative overture, Aria called out, "Brandy? We're here to help you."

Grayson kept his breath shallow, as if by breathing deeply, he'd scare away the already-frightened woman. "I'm coming on board. I brought my friend. You can trust her."

His boots clomped along the gangplank, no need for silence now. He reached the bow of the boat where a stepladder nestled against the fiberglass. Planting one foot on the step, he peeked over the side. "Brandy?"

The empty cushions and bolted-down tables rocked back and forth with the sway of the boat. "Maybe she's not here yet. Maybe she changed her mind."

Aria materialized behind him and he jumped when she touched his back. "This must be the boat the blah—the women were using to smuggle the drugs into Canada. I can see it. Festively decorated for the holidays, eight to ten people heading over for the day or longer. How'd they get the drugs into Point Edward?"

Grayson grabbed onto the railings and pulled himself into the boat. He kicked the side of a refrigerator with the toe of his work boot. "Refreshments and everything."

Aria pranced up the steps, as lithe as a cat, and squeezed past him to the fridge. She flipped up the lid. "Drinks, snacks. They had a whole operation to cover their…operation."

"Do you hear that?" Grayson cocked his head to take in the sound of rhythmic tapping, something hard against the fiberglass of the boat. The noise kept time with the undulations of the boat.

"What is that?" Aria let the lid of the fridge fall and stood with her chin lifted. "It's coming from the side of the boat in the water."

Aria shuffled to the starboard of the boat and peered over the edge. "Grayson."

Her stark tone had him lunging to her side. As he

gazed into the water, Brandy's white face, looking like a reflection of the moon, stared back at him. The zipper on her jacket kept hitting the side of the boat saying, *I'm here, I'm here, I'm here.*

Chapter Twelve

Aria glanced in her rearview mirror to make sure no-body from the TCD team was following her—not that they would be. After she'd called 9-1-1, she'd called Alana, and most of the team had converged on the ma-rina a few minutes after the PHPD first responders.

The local cops deferred to the FBI to process the crime scene once Alana had convinced them the mur-der was tied to their Blah Boatie case. Aria hated that they'd chosen "Blah Boatie" for the nickname, hated it for Grayson and all the other families of the dead women, but it fit and so it stayed.

Alana had cited case confidentiality when the lead PHPD cop on the scene asked Aria how she'd happened to be at the marina and found the dead woman. Aria had told Alana about how Brandy had contacted Gray-son and why.

She had also shooed Grayson away from the scene before the PHPD arrived. He was proving too valuable at the docks to have the cops blow his cover. Alana had approved of her decision.

Alana probably wouldn't approve of this decision, though.

At this point, Aria had to trust her gut. Grayson needed to know what they'd found on the boat, and just maybe he needed her.

The look on his face when he'd realized Brandy was dead in the water had bruised her heart. He'd just had to identify his own sister, and another dead woman was staring him in the face—literally staring him in the face with her dead, brown eyes. Another woman who'd trusted him.

Her foot heavy on the accelerator, she made the next turn faster than she'd intended, the tires squealing to hurry her on. The car bounced as she pulled into the parking lot of Grayson's motel and wheeled into a space.

She scrambled from the car and half jogged to his room. The door flew open before she could knock, and he pulled her inside.

"Should you be here?" A pair of dark blue sweats hung low on his hips and droplets of water glistened in the hair sprinkled across his bare chest.

"Maybe not, but I had to see you after what happened." She crossed her arms, hugging herself when she really wanted to hug him.

He ran a hand through his hair, the wet ends flipping up. "I don't get it. Was she another blah boatie? Tony's in jail. Did they order another hit man to pick up where he left off?"

"She wasn't killed like the others. This is something else." Aria perched on the arm of the threadbare sofa. "Brandy didn't have any ID on her, wasn't carrying any drugs. She didn't die from a bullet wound to the chest. This was meant to look like an accidental drowning."

"Oh, my God." Grayson dug two fingers into his temple. "They knew she was going to squeal, didn't they?"

"They must have. If they'd suspected her of stealing drugs or money, she would've died like the others."

"Do you think they know she went there to meet me? Do you think someone was watching us as we boarded the boat and found her?" He paced to the window and cracked the blinds, which hung down on one side.

"I don't know. Did you see or hear anyone around before I got there?" She yanked a damp towel draped across the back of the sofa and walked toward him slowly, holding it out. "I interrupted your shower. You're still wet."

"I was just getting out when I heard a car drive into the parking lot. In case it was Brandy's killer coming for me, I didn't want to meet him naked and unprepared." He pulled a Glock from the pocket of his baggy sweats. "Don't worry, Special Agent Calletti, it's registered and I have a permit to carry."

"I don't care at this point. If the killer saw you at the marina, you'll need protection." She bunched up the towel and pushed it against his chest. "And you need to dry off. You'll get a chill."

He set his gun down on the table by the front door and took the towel from her. He wiped it across his chest and cranked up the heater underneath the window, giving it a kick with the side of his foot at the same time.

"Were you able to convince the rest of your team to keep my name out of this?"

"It didn't take much convincing. My director understands the importance of maintaining your cover. We told the PHPD that we had an informant who led me to that boat…and wait until I tell you about that boat."

"You mean *Fun Times* doesn't live up to its name?" He hung the towel around his neck and two-stepped past her. "Let me get a sweatshirt."

He disappeared into the other room and emerged, yanking a white T-shirt over his head. "That heater is surprisingly efficient."

He didn't have to tell her that. In the short time she'd been standing with her back to it, her body temperature had risen several degrees…unless she could attribute that to watching Grayson saunter across the room, his sweats slipping a little lower with each step.

He patted the back of the sofa. "Sit down and tell me what happened. Take off your jacket. You look like you're about to keel over from heat exhaustion."

She shrugged out of her maroon jacket with the fur-lined hood, the gun in her pocket banging against her leg. She hung it on the back of a chair with a cigarette burn in its blue-plaid cushion.

She lowered herself to the sofa, next to Grayson, sitting on the edge. "You know those drinks we saw in that fridge?"

"Yeah, first-class all the way."

"They were fake. All the containers were faked with false bottoms or hollowed out."

Grayson whistled. "For drugs?"

"That's what we think. The Maddie Johnsons picked up drugs somewhere on the US side, perhaps already packed in these containers, or they did that themselves when they got on board the *Fun Times*. Then the sellers hopped on for their pleasure cruise across the river to Canada, got served refreshments, disembarked in Point Edward, carrying their fake snacks, and distributed the drugs there. The women then came back to this side, ready for another shipment and another cruise."

"Except some of them got greedy, including Chloe."

"We don't know that for sure. We only have Tony's word."

Grayson shifted on the sofa and she dipped toward him, her shoulder bumping his. "To think I was working alongside Tony, and all this time he was a stone-cold killer. His uncle's a good guy. Tony's arrest is going to hit him hard. Do they know yet? Does Tony's family know?"

"We're not releasing his arrest yet. We don't want to tip anyone off, and Tony isn't all that anxious for word to get out that he's in custody. We need to convince him the only way he's going to keep safe is if he gives up the name of the kingpin in exchange for our protection. We're not going to protect him otherwise. We have his confession and, once the guys at the top realize we have their hit man, Tony's in trouble whether he tells us anything or not."

"You're going to make it in his best interest to cough up the name."

"Or as much as he knows. But at least we've grounded *Fun Times*, putting a crimp in their smuggling business for now. They'll have to look for another way to get their drugs to Canada."

"What about those tunnels? They stashing the drugs there?"

"That's what we think."

"If they're near the docks, I can do a little digging—not literally—and see what I can find out." Grayson wedged a bare foot on the rickety table in front of them.

"You don't have to do anything else, Grayson. You've done enough. You lost your sister and still you identified the killer for us, and then you managed to discover the smuggling boat." She folded her hands around one knee, her fingers fidgety. "You can hang up your career in law enforcement and go back to Detroit…wait for Danny to come to you and give him the kind of life Chloe never could."

"Is that what you want?" His warm hand covered hers, stilling her agitated fingers. "Do you want me to go back to Detroit? Leave Port Huron? Leave you?"

His words hung in the air between them and she took little sips of air, afraid to disturb the words, preferring to let them float just within her grasp, preferring to believe in dreams.

"Do you want me to leave you, Aria?" He slid his hand upward and circled her wrist with his fingers. "Because I don't want to leave you."

Her lashes fluttered as she swallowed, afraid to meet his eyes. She spoke to the strong fingers that had her in a light clasp that felt like vise around her heart. "I… you… I've been here for you, that's all this is. You're caught up in this moment. You just lost your sister.

Your life will return to normal soon, although you'll always mourn your sister, but this is my life, Grayson. I'll go on to the next case, the next victims, the next victims' families."

He released her and jumped up from the sofa, turning his back on her. "Is that what I am to you? Another grieving family member? Someone to pity, humor, maybe use?"

His accusation twisted a knife in her heart and she sprang up from the sofa and grabbed the back of his T-shirt, her fingers skimming his smooth back. "Absolutely not. If you could've heard me at war with myself on the drive over here, excoriating myself for being unprofessional and then letting those warnings fly out the window as my heart took over."

Grayson turned slowly and she was sucked into the depths of his blue eyes, as dark as Lake Huron on a stormy day. "You're here. Your heart won."

She parted her lips to protest, to object, to regain her stature as an officer of the law. Instead, her mouth invited his kiss and he pulled her into his arms and sealed his lips over hers.

Her body molded to his, as if their parts fit together like some well-oiled piece of machinery. But his hands on her back, beneath her shirt, sliding over her skin, felt purely human.

In danger of melting into a puddle at his feet, she curled one arm around his neck and the other around his waist, pulling him closer.

As his pelvis thrust against her, he prodded her with his erection, hard and unrestrained beneath his loose sweats. She slipped her hand beneath the elastic waist-band, her palm skimming the solid muscle of his back-side.

Without breaking their kiss, Grayson reached up and released the clasp of her bra. He then stepped back to create a whisper of space between them and his hand traveled to her breast, cupping it with one roughened palm. He circled her tingling nipple with the pad of his thumb as he deepened their kiss even more to the point where she couldn't tell where the outline of her body left off and his began.

She moved her hips against his in a slow, sensu-ous dance, and he rocked with her, the wordless song playing in both of their heads, new to them but oddly familiar.

His lips left hers and continued their path of discov-ery across her face to her ear. He flicked her lobe with his tongue and then planted a new trail of kisses down her throat, his teeth grazing her collarbone.

She wanted him more than she'd ever wanted any-thing in her life. Wanted him to take a piece of her, as surely as she wanted a piece of him.

But right now that logic she'd thrown out the window on her rush over here had seeped beneath the door of the motel room, had started curling around her heart, causing a chill between them.

Touching his forehead to hers, Grayson cupped her face in his hands. "I'm sorry."

His gruff voice, ragged with passion, pricked her with shame.

"You don't have to apologize. I wanted you...still want you, but..."

He put a finger to her lips. "You don't have to explain anything. I got carried away—we both did. There's this thing between us. At least tell me you feel that."

"I do." She turned her head and pressed her throbbing lips against his palm. "Why do you think I flew over here?"

"To tell me about the boat?" He stepped back from her and the space between them felt like an ocean. He smiled and kissed her forehead. "You'd better put yourself together and get going. You still have a lot of work to do on this case, but I'm not going anywhere, Aria."

"I don't want you to." She twisted her arms behind her to clasp her bra, giving it about three tries before Grayson said, "Turn around."

She presented her back to him and he pulled up her top and hooked her bra. He even ran his fingers through her tangled hair.

"There, you're Special Agent Aria Calletti again."

She twirled around and, with a catch in her voice, said, "And I always will be."

ALANA CRACKED OPEN the car door of her rental and dropped the half-smoked cigarette on the ground. She stuck one leg out of the car and ground the butt with the toe of her boot. Then she leaned over, pinched it between two fingers and dropped it in a plastic bag.

When she shut the door, she waved the fumes out the window before rolling it up against the chill. Two and a half cigarettes this week—not bad, considering this case.

The motel door she'd been watching for the past half hour opened and two figures stood in silhouette within the frame. The taller one bent toward the shorter one, their shadows merging for a second in a good-night kiss.

Alana narrowed her eyes as she watched Aria float through the parking lot toward the blue sedan. Grayson Rhodes stood at the door of his room, also focused on Aria until she got into her car. The guy had a protective streak a mile long. Too bad he hadn't been able to save his sister.

But then his sister was an addict. You couldn't save an addict. Isn't that what they always told you?

Alana sniffed and wiped her nose with a tissue. Damned smoke. She'd almost given up the filthy habit completely but some days, some cases… She shrugged.

If Steve ever caught her, he'd read her the riot act. They'd quit smoking together and, as far as she knew, her husband had stayed nicotine-free. But you couldn't force people to give up their vices. Isn't that also what they always told you?

Sneak smoking was the only secret she had kept from Steve. She'd confessed her biggest one to him before they'd married. When she'd told Steve about the child she'd had at eighteen and given up for adoption, he hadn't blinked an eye. He told her he'd support her in whatever way she needed, even if she wanted to reach out to Tania—at least, that's what her adoptive parents had named her. To Alana, she'd always be Miko.

With open adoptions, she'd always hoped Miko

would try to find her. Alana and Steve had never had children together. He had two sons from a previous marriage; high-school-age boys when she and Steve had gotten married. Neither she nor Steve had the career to accommodate a baby, maintaining a marriage was hard enough.

She'd accepted it...because she'd always believed one day Miko would find her. But her daughter had never made the effort. Alana knew all about Miko though, tracked her, followed her through social media, relished in her successes, agonized over her failures—all her failures.

Alana blinked and blew her nose. She cranked on the engine, although Aria was long gone from the parking lot. So, the new agent was falling for a victim's brother on a case. Should she warn her? Reprimand her?

Alana pulled out another cigarette and rolled down the window. Who was she to give personal advice?

Chapter Thirteen

Aria shivered, teeth chattering, as she watched Max pull up his wetsuit and squeeze his arms into the sleeves. He reached over his head, grabbed the cord on the zipper and secured himself inside the neoprene, which couldn't really be airtight enough to keep out the cold waters of Lake Huron.

A few of the dockworkers had gathered on the next pier over to watch the FBI's activity, but they couldn't possibly know what was going on. Rihanna had released nothing to the media regarding tunnels under the water, near the docks.

Now Rihanna stood near the roped-off entrance to the dock, sharp and elegant in a belted raincoat, her appearance deceiving the few members of the press craning their necks toward the action, trying to get a story. If they thought Rihanna would let anything slip about this procedure on the docks, they had the wrong woman.

Once Tony had mentioned tunnels, Opaline and Max had delved into old plans for Port Huron and the docks. They'd discovered some blueprints for underwater tunnels supposedly created during World War II.

So far, what Tony had revealed to her and Axel during the interrogation was panning out. They just needed one more vital piece of evidence from him.

Aria twisted her head around, pretending to brush off a few raindrops from the shoulder of her FBI jacket, but really sneaking a peek at the dockworkers. Was Grayson among them?

She'd almost succumbed to her desires last night. What would Alana think of her if she knew she'd gotten entangled with a victim's brother on her first case?

As if conjured from her thoughts, Alana appeared at Aria's side and rubbed her back. "Are you doing okay? Better Max than us, right?"

"I can't even fathom what it's going to feel like for him once he slips into that icy water. And I'm fine. You?" Aria raised her brows at her boss, the question not altogether idle.

The dark circles beneath Alana's eyes had added a few years to the otherwise ageless director's appearance, her brisk step a little slower this morning.

"I never sleep well in hotel rooms. Although my husband and I spend a lot of time apart, I do miss his company at night when I'm on the road." Alana squeezed her arm. "In this job, it's good to have someone to come home to, Aria."

"Alana!" Max waved his arms over his head. "I'm ready."

Aria sucked in her bottom lip as she watched Alana stride toward Max at the water's edge, squaring her shoulders, putting back on her military strut as if it were a jacket she'd momentarily shrugged off.

Then she caught up with her just as Alana clipped an underwater camera to Max's weight belt. "If you see anything of interest down there, take some pictures."

Two members of the PHPD dive team were accompanying him under water—not that Max would do anything as foolish as paddling into a tunnel on his own, but he was an experienced diver and experienced divers never went solo.

As Aria watched the three divers slide into the dark water, her phone buzzed. She pulled it out of her pocket and glanced at it.

Alana asked, "Any news?"

"It's a text from Rihanna."

"The Rihanna standing right over there, keeping the press at bay?" Alana pointed at Rihanna, who was giving Aria a thumbs-up sign.

Aria cupped the phone in her hand and reread Rihanna's message as her heart soared, a smile curving her lips.

"Ah, good news." Alana crossed her arms and wedged one foot against a wooden stump.

"CPS is allowing Grayson Rhodes to visit his nephew, and the foster parents have agreed and invited him over tonight." Despite the frosty bite in the air, Aria felt her cheeks warm.

If she'd known Alana was going to question her about the text, she never would've been so transparently happy. Who was she actually kidding? She wouldn't have been able to control herself one way or the other. If Rihanna had walked over here and told her in person, she probably would've hugged her.

Alana dipped her head once. "You should go with him."

"M-me?" Aria clasped the phone between her two hands like an ecstatic schoolgirl, and then dropped the phone back in her pocket. "Shouldn't Rihanna go with him? She's already met the foster parents."

"Rhodes trusts you. You've been his contact through all this. You were there when he ID'd his sister. The two of you discovered Brandy's body last night." Alana crossed her fingers. "There's a connection between you."

"Okay, I'll call him later and set it up."

A squad car pulled up and Opaline emerged from the back seat, pulling the fur-lined hood of her pink jacket over her head. She bent forward, leaning her head in the passenger window and chatting with the officer before spinning around and picking her way across the wooden planks of the dock in her high-heeled boots with fur at the top to match her hood.

"It's freezing out here." Opaline pulled on a pair of mittens.

"You don't have to be out here. You did enough work finding the plans for the tunnels." Alana peered around Opaline's shoulder at the cop car. "Special delivery service?"

"Oh, that's Gordon. He was coming this way and offered me a lift." Leaning forward, Opaline cupped her mouth and whispered, "He likes cats."

"So did your ex." Alana chuckled and wandered toward the water.

Opaline stared after Alana for a few seconds and said, "Is she okay?"

"She looks tired, doesn't she?"

"She does, but I hope you didn't tell her that." Opaline jerked her thumb over her shoulder. "How long have Max and the other divers been below?"

"Just about ten minutes. They're going to need hot coffee and warm showers when they get out." Aria hunched her shoulders. "I hope they find something. Do you know why the government built those tunnels?"

"Munitions. Maybe they thought the Germans were going to attack the US via the Great Lakes. Unfortunately for us, the plans we saw didn't have the land endpoints—just the construction of the tunnels beneath the water. I think we were missing some maps or plans."

"Maybe Max can find those points and those will lead us to the drug storage area. All three bodies were discovered near the lake. When the hit on them was put out, their locations weren't a secret. The women weren't killed in their apartments or their cars. They were alone on those roads near the lake, for some reason. One even had her baby with her." Aria pressed a hand to her heart.

"Picking up their stash for the trip to Canada. I think we can shut this down, but we need to get the person at the top because he'll just set up shop somewhere else, using other resources, other people, to get his product across the border." Opaline pushed her hood back from her face, the blue ends of her hair clinging to the fur. "Do you think Tony Balducci will give up the top dog?"

"Axel seems to think so, and I have faith in him."

"Uh-oh." Opaline peered over Aria's shoulder. "Looks like it's lunchtime for the boys on the dock. I hope they don't come nosing around here. Maybe Gordon can ward them off while Rihanna keeps the press at bay."

"They've been eyeballing us all morning, but the PHPD has us cordoned off." Aria's phone buzzed in her pocket and she pulled it out. She read Grayson's text, asking if she could talk.

She tipped her phone back and forth at Opaline. "I need to make a call. Excuse me for a sec."

"Go ahead. I'm going to see what Alana knows...or at least see if she needs any coffee."

Aria moved away from the staging area for the divers and called Grayson. He barely let one ring finish before he answered.

"What's happening over there?"

"We have divers looking for those underwater tunnels. We think the drugs might be hidden there."

"I hope you find them, get them off the streets."

"What's the talk at the docks?"

"Everything from you guys found another body to it actually being Tony's body."

Aria drew in a breath. "Tony hasn't reached out to his family yet?"

"Nope, or Chuck's not telling me. Is that good or bad?"

"It's good. It means Tony's afraid of reprisals and we can use that to get him to talk. Without our protection on the inside, he's toast." With the back of her hand,

Aria dashed away a raindrop that had hit her cheek. "I have some other news for you—good news."

"I could use some about now."

Aria gripped the phone in her hand as butterflies swirled in her stomach. Was he referring to the way she'd shut him down last night?

She rushed to fill the expectant silence. "If you're free tonight, you can visit Danny."

His excited words burst over the phone. "Are you serious? I can see my nephew?"

"DCS approved it and the foster parents agreed—six o'clock tonight, and I'm going with you."

"I'm glad it's you." Grayson had lowered his voice and the tone sent a delicious thrill curling through her body. "Look, last night…"

She held up her hand, as if he could see her. "Don't. It's all right."

"Okay, good. I'm going to eat my lunch. Do you want to pick me up tonight at my luxurious motel? I get off at five, and I'll head back, shower and change."

"I can do that. Can you be ready by around five forty?"

"I can. And… Aria?"

"Yes?" She couldn't control the breathlessness of her voice or the fluttering of her heart when Grayson said her name.

"I'm glad we didn't make love last night in that dump. When we come together, it's going to be something special."

He ended the call before she could reply to his outrageous statement. So, that's why he'd said it was all right that they hadn't continued down the path their touching and kissing would've surely led them. He'd figured their union was inevitable anyway, and he could bide his time for the right moment.

Was he wrong?

Alana whooped. "They're coming up."

Stashing her phone, Aria rushed to the water's edge where the rope that had followed the divers down was now taut and vibrating.

Her heart lodged in her throat until the first diver's mask broke the surface. As Max clambered out of the brackish lake, water sluicing off his prosthetic, he ran a finger across his throat.

Aria grabbed Alana's elbow. "They didn't find anything?"

"Let's wait and see."

As the divers sat on the wooden stumps that littered the dock, removing their fins and masks, Opaline scurried up with a cardboard drink holder containing three cups of coffee.

When Max emerged from his mask and accepted a coffee from Opaline, Aria followed Alana to his side.

He brushed a hand over his head. "Damn, that's cold."

"What did you see, Max?"

He unhooked the camera from his belt and dangled it from his fingers. "It's all on here. We did find the entrance to one tunnel, so they still exist, but the door is either locked or rusted shut. There's no way we can get in there."

Alana smacked a fist in her palm. "But we know

they exist and Tony's story isn't a lie. The exits on the land must be somewhere, and I'm guessing they're near where the bodies were found. What else were those women doing there by themselves?"

"We searched those sites for evidence. Now we need to search the surrounding locations for possible hidey-holes for the drugs." Max slipped a fin off his prosthetic.

Turning to Aria, Alana said, "I'm going to get Selena and Blanca on that, and I want you to go with her, Aria, so you can see how the K-9 tracker works."

"I'd like that."

"I got some more good news for Mr. Rhodes. Carly called me with the toxicology and DNA results on mother and baby. Danny is Chloe Larsen's child, which we knew, anyway, but he didn't have any drugs in his system at all. Chloe, on the other hand…" Alana stopped and turned her head to the side. She dragged a tissue from her pocket, dabbed her eyes and wiped it across her nose. "Sorry, damn cold. Chloe, on the other hand, had a small quantity of opioids in her system."

Max peeled down the top of his wetsuit. "Damn, that girl was on the highway to hell."

Aria put her hand on Alana's stiff back. "It's been a raw morning out here, and it's starting to rain. Why don't you go back to the hotel and put your feet up for a few hours? We all know what we're doing."

"Nonsense." Alana flipped up the hood on her FBI jacket. "I'm going back to the war room, and Opaline's going to blow up these underwater pictures Max took. I suggest you and Selena join us. You too, Max."

"As soon as I get some warm clothes and a hot

lunch." He raised a hand to the other divers. "Thanks, guys. I'll buy you some chili."

Alana had hurried away and hopped into her rental, taking off after a few words with the PD.

Aria tapped Opaline's shoulder. "Hey, Opaline. Do you think your hot cop can give me a lift back to the station in his squad car? Alana must've forgotten she was my ride."

"Yeah, she sure was in a big hurry to get out of here."

Aria stared after Alana's rental as it zipped around the corner and out of sight. It didn't take any investigative skills to know Alana didn't have a cold. Those had been tears in the usually stoic director's eyes.

When Grayson got off work, he rushed to a store, where he bought a stuffed tiger and a saucer-shaped contraption for the baby to sit in and entertain himself with the little gadgets and dials along the tray that encircled the seat. He hoped the foster parents didn't mind, but every time he'd seen Danny in the past, he'd come bearing gifts—and diapers, and diaper wipes, and clothes, and even big-ticket items like that car seat Danny had been found in next to his mother's dead body.

By the time Aria drove up to his motel, he'd showered and changed into a pair of jeans and a flannel shirt and was standing outside his room with the tiger under one arm and the saucer at his feet.

Her eyes widened when she saw him. She parked and then slid from behind the wheel. "You come prepared."

"I always bring Danny something when I see him."

He picked up the saucer by the edge. "Do you have room for this?"

"You can wedge it in the back seat." She yanked open the door for him and he turned the saucer seat on its side and shoved it into the back.

He climbed in next to her in her car, clutching the tiger in his lap. "The foster parents are okay with this?"

"Rihanna said they were thrilled that Danny had an uncle who wanted him. She said they're incredible people."

"They must be." Unlike Danny's mother. He stroked the tiger's ear with his thumb.

"Don't get too attached to that tiger." Aria tugged on the toy's tail before she pulled out of the motel's parking lot. "You're going to have to fight Danny for it."

He stretched his lips into a smile. He didn't know why his nerves were jangling. Either he was afraid Danny would reject him…or that Aria would.

He tossed the tiger into the back seat. "Nothing came from the search for the tunnels today?"

"Max found an underwater tunnel, but the entrance was locked. We have no way of knowing where it pops up on land."

"Probably where the women were murdered. Why else would they be walking in those areas at night by themselves?"

"Exactly. I'm going out with our K-9 agent and her dog tomorrow. The handler will give the dog something belonging to the victims to sniff and see if she can track them."

Aria's GPS spit out some directions and she joined the highway traffic. "It's not far, maybe ten minutes."

"Did Rihanna indicate when the DNA results would be in?"

"Shouldn't be much longer because…" She lodged the tip of her tongue in the corner of her mouth and flicked on her turn signal.

"Because what?"

"We got other test results back, which confirmed that Chloe and Danny were mother and son, and that Danny didn't have any drugs in his system."

Grayson blew out a breath. "Yeah, I could've told you that. I grilled Chloe on that score and, while she didn't always answer my questions, when she did, she told the truth. You're leaving something out."

Aria's hands tightened on the steering wheel and she shot him a glance from the corner of her eye. "Toxicology came back on Chloe, too."

"Let me guess." His eye twitched. "She had drugs in her system."

"Opioids."

Grayson's hands curled into fists, despite himself. "I could've told you that, too."

He stared out the window at the scenery rushing past, draped in gray, thinking about all the times he'd tried to get Chloe to stop using. The last time had been before her pregnancy when he'd sent her to a high-end, live-in treatment center. She'd lasted two weeks before running off with some musician. That guy could even be Danny's father, but if Chloe hadn't mentioned it to her fellow escapee, Grayson had no intention of suggesting to this guy that he might be a dad. Grayson wanted Danny to have a good life. From here on out, sunshine and…tigers.

"We're on the street." Aria tapped the window. "Nice homes."

She pulled up in front of a house that had a midsize SUV and a red truck parked in the driveway. "Ready?"

"Oh, yeah." He had the door open before she cut the engine. Ducking into the back seat, he grabbed the toys and marched up to the porch, Aria tailing behind him.

The door swung open before he had a chance to knock, and a man whose shoulders practically spanned the doorway stuck out his hand. "Rich Colby. You must be Danny's uncle. Same blue eyes, same expression when someone tries to take one of his toys away."

I must look ready to do battle or something. Grayson puffed out a breath and, with the tiger under his arm, shook the man's hand. "Grayson Rhodes, and I can't tell you how much it means to me that you took in Danny."

A woman with fluffy blond hair peeped over her husband's shoulder. "You do look like Danny. I'm Sarah Colby. C'mon in."

"I'm sorry." Grayson turned to Aria. "This is Special Agent Aria Calletti with the FBI."

While Aria shook hands with the Colbys as they stood in the entryway, Grayson dropped the toys on the floor and made a beeline for his nephew, standing in the playpen across the room, his hands curled on the side, swaying back and forth.

"Hey, buddy. Do you remember your uncle Grayson?"

He swept the boy up and pressed his nose against Danny's soft hair, a towhead, just like Chloe was as a baby.

Danny's legs wrapped around Grayson's waist and he patted his face with sticky hands.

Grayson's nose stung and he bounced Danny in his arms for a few seconds before turning around and facing Aria and the Colbys. "I think he remembers me."

"Of course, he does." Sarah beamed. "He's totally comfortable with you. That DNA test is just a formality. DCS has to be sure before they release a baby. My guess is you'll have him by Christmas."

Danny seemed to approve as he squealed and kicked his legs against Grayson's hip.

Aria rescued the stuffed animal from the floor and waved him in the air. "Did you see the tiger Uncle Grayson brought you?"

Danny chuckled and reached out for the toy.

Grayson squatted on the floor near the play mat. "He's crawling, isn't he? I—I haven't seen him for a few months, but the last time I talked to my sister, she said he'd started crawling."

"Crawling, rolling, pulling himself up to standing and almost cruising." Sarah put her head to one side, looking like a feathered bird. "You're going to have your hands full, Grayson. Are you married?"

"I'm not, but I'm my own boss and I can work from home. And I'll be hiring a nanny."

Rich snorted. "I don't have to tell you, Sarah already looked you up online, so we know you're in a good financial position to care for the boy."

"I am, but it's more than that. I want to make up for… everything he lost."

"I'm sure you will." Sarah sniffled and dabbed the corner of her eye with her fingertip. "Do either of you want anything to drink?"

"No, thanks." Grayson had put Danny on the play mat and handed him the tiger, which he was now squishing between his arms.

"Just some water for me." Aria sat beside Grayson, tucking her legs beneath her and waving at Danny.

Danny dropped the tiger and reached out for Aria. She pulled him into her lap, facing him toward Grayson, wrapping one arm around his belly and bouncing him, while he giggled.

Sarah returned with a glass of water for Aria, which she placed on the coffee table next to her. "You look like you can handle a baby."

"I have four brothers, and they all have children. I have a plethora of nieces and nephews, and I've filled in as a babysitter more times than I can count."

"You should find a nanny like Aria, Grayson." Sarah's gaze darted back and forth between them. "We'll give you some time alone with Danny, and then it's bedtime for this little guy."

Sarah wasn't wrong. Aria was a natural with Danny. Maybe she reminded his nephew of his mother. She made Danny laugh, and Grayson caught himself more than once with a big, goofy grin on his own face. Aria obviously had the gift to charm the Rhodes men.

Grayson watched Aria holding Danny's hands as

he stood, rocking back and forth. She'd make a great mother someday.

"What?" She tilted her head and Danny made a grab for her hair. "You're looking at me like you're trying to figure me out."

Could he be more obvious?

"Four brothers, huh? That must've been a challenge for you."

"In a way. They're very protective—all firefighters."

What a gauntlet for any man to walk who wanted to date Aria. "Your father, too?"

"My dad was an autoworker for a while—got laid off."

"Familiar story."

"My mother was a police officer before she had my oldest brother. When Dad got laid off, Mom wanted to go back to work, but he wouldn't allow it." Her jawline hardened and her eyes narrowed. "Can you believe that? Stubborn, macho nonsense."

"That's…yeah, doesn't make much sense."

His inadequate response got lost in Danny's giggles as he plopped onto his bottom. He'd have to thank his nephew for that bit of intervention later.

After about thirty minutes, the Colbys crept back into the room discreetly. "Is he starting to get a little fussy?"

"Maybe a little wound up." Aria pushed to her feet, leaving Danny clinging to Grayson's arm as he tried out his sea legs. "Say good-night to your uncle, Danny. Your new daddy."

Grayson pulled Danny against his chest and stood

with him wrapped around his body like a baby chimp, as Aria chatted with the Colbys by the front door. He kissed the side of Danny's head and whispered, "Be a good boy for Rich and Sarah, and then I'm coming back for you, Danny... I'm coming back for you for your mom's sake."

As Aria pulled away from the Colby house, Grayson said, "Wow, they're just about perfect, aren't they?"

"Danny couldn't ask for a better set of foster parents." She patted his thigh and his knee jerked. "But Danny is obviously taken with his uncle. You'll do fine."

"He was obviously taken with you, too." *Like uncle, like nephew.*

He kept that thought to himself. He'd already come on too strong over the phone today, telling her how and when he planned to make love to her. He always got what he wanted, and he'd never wanted anything more in his life than Aria Calletti. But she was not his for the taking—no matter how soft her lips looked when she talked to him or how her dark brown eyes turned to liquid when they met his.

"Well, yeah, I do have all those nieces and nephews, and I'm not kidding when I say my brothers use me as a babysitting service." She snapped her fingers. "Speaking of which, you should start looking for a nanny... or a wife."

He raised one eyebrow at her. Did she really want him to find a wife? He remembered her saying how she'd move on to the next case, the next victim, after this. He'd hoped she was convincing herself, but maybe he was the one who needed convincing that she just didn't see any future for them beyond this investigation. It stung.

He ignored her suggestion and gazed out the window as she fiddled with the radio, turning it up to fill the now awkward silence between them. She even sang along, making things even more awkward.

Grayson actually blew out a sigh of relief when she pulled into the motel parking lot and turned down the radio. She laughed. "Home sweet home."

"That it is." He opened his door and turned toward her before she could cut the engine. "Thanks, Aria. Thanks for coming with me and thanks for pushing for the meeting."

"I…"

"I know it was you, and I appreciate it." He got out of the car and leaned back in. "I'll keep my eyes and ears open on the dock."

He shut the door and walked to his room, listening for her car to take off, not wanting to turn around. They couldn't have a repeat of what happened last night. Maybe she didn't even want a repeat if she was suggesting he find himself a wife. He had misread her, had thought she felt something she didn't feel.

Instead of driving away, she turned off the ignition. He kept trudging to his door, hoping she'd think better of it.

He pulled out his key, but he didn't have to use it. The door had been kicked in. He pushed it open and a knot formed in his gut as he surveyed the room.

Shoving his hand in his pocket, he curled his fingers around the handle of his gun.

When Aria's boots tapped against the concrete walkway, he turned to her. "Stay back."

Her eyes popped open. "What's wrong?"

"Someone broke into my room and tossed the place. I've been made."

Chapter Fourteen

A sharp spike of adrenaline made Aria dizzy and she licked her dry lips. Why was Grayson telling her to stay back? He was the civilian here.

He held out his hand to her and withdrew his weapon from his pocket. "Let me make sure he's gone."

She pulled her own gun out of her purse and spun around toward the parking lot. Was the intruder still there? Watching them?

A minute later, Grayson poked his head out the door. "All clear. All clear out there, too?"

"I didn't see anyone, and nobody started a car, but that doesn't mean he's not still there, watching."

"We won't give him anything to watch. Come on in."

She shoved her gun into the side pocket of her purse, dropped it by the door and brushed past him into the room. She widened her eyes and gulped. "You're not kidding. Someone did a number on this room."

Her gaze traveled from the upended sofa cushions to the gaping drawers in the compact kitchen, spilling their guts to the books and papers on the floor. She didn't even want to look in the bedroom.

"Closets in the bedroom? Clothes? Suitcase?"

"Same." He grabbed a cushion from the floor and tossed it onto the sofa.

"Did you have anything in here to tie you to Chloe or Danny? Anything with your real name on it?"

He patted his pockets. "I have my phone on me, my wallet. I didn't bring a laptop. Any pictures I have are on my phone. I didn't keep any receipts from the motel or anywhere else. But even if they don't know what my connection is to this case, someone has figured out I'm not the new dockworker hoping to make a home in Port Huron…unless this is some random break-in."

"While this isn't the best area in town, there are no coincidences. You were targeted. Someone saw us together."

"Or it could be that someone knew Brandy reached out to me. Maybe this drug ring thinks Brandy told me something."

Aria balled a fist against her stomach, which had started churning. That notion worried her even more than if someone just thought Grayson was working with the FBI or was some kind of informant.

She swallowed, which was more like a gulp. "If the drug dealer running the show thinks you know something about the operation, know something about him, your life is in danger."

"If he thought Brandy already spilled her guts to me, they wouldn't have killed her. Or they would've waited at the marina and killed us both."

"We don't know that, Grayson." She pressed her folded hands against her chin. "You should leave Port

Huron. Quit the job and leave. When Danny is released to you, you can come back and pick him up, but it's time for you to stop this game you're playing."

"I'm not going anywhere." He took her by the shoulders. "And you don't have to worry about me. I haven't had anyone worry about me since my dad died."

"You're not going back to work, are you? You don't have to pretend anymore. You can move out of this dump, at least." He was in danger now, and she worried that he didn't understand the breadth of the risk. These drug dealers didn't fool around.

"This dump?" He released her and spread his arms. "I'm getting kind of used to it, and I'm not quitting the job. I'm going to carry on as if nothing happened. Let them wonder about me. Let them wonder what I'm doing here."

"Grayson! They won't wonder. That's the problem. They'll act. And we've both seen what that looks like." She ducked and shoved a cushion into place on the sofa, trying to keep her emotions under control by not looking at him. "Do you always get what you want?"

"Almost always."

The low, sultry tone of his voice made her heart flutter just a little, and she was afraid to turn around. She patted the cushion and picked up the next one.

"Why did you follow me inside?" He righted a table and stacked his books on top of it. "I thought you left after you dropped me off."

She smoothed her hand over the threadbare couch, letting her hair fall around her face like a curtain. She'd run after him because she'd felt empty inside when he'd left her. She'd run after him to tell him not to find a mother for Danny. She'd run after him because, after pushing him away, she wanted him close again.

"You know, in all the excitement, I forgot what I was going to tell you."

"You don't have to help me clean up." He snatched up her purse from the floor by the door where she'd dropped it and swung it next to her. "You have another busy day tomorrow, and I have to work."

She took the purse from him and hitched it over her shoulder. "I can't convince you to give this pretense up, can I?"

He smiled. "No."

She stared at him, thinking how different he was. He was wealthy enough to have hired a private detective to look into his sister's disappearance, but he'd taken on the task himself, unafraid of where that might lead him. Now that he knew Chloe was dead, he still wouldn't let go until her killers were all rounded up. It was futile to try to convince him otherwise.

"Let me know if you discover anything missing," she said, resigned to his insistence on staying involved.

"Yes, ma'am, and I'll walk you out to your car—just in case."

Crossing her arms, she said, "You do understand that I'm an armed FBI agent, right?"

"Oh, I know that, ma'am. You never let me forget it." He walked to the door and swept it open. "Almost never."

She brushed a hand across her cheek, as if trying to brush away the warmth creeping across her skin. "I'm just saying, if I don't have to worry about you, you certainly don't have to worry about me."

"I know I don't have to." He flicked the broken wood in the doorjamb. "I'm going to have to visit Bernie in the management office to see if he can put a lock on tonight and fix this tomorrow."

Grayson walked her to the car and stood in the parking lot, watching her drive away. When he no longer appeared in her rearview mirror, she slumped behind the wheel.

How had she fallen so fast and so hard for Grayson Rhodes? The man wasn't even her type—gorgeous, successful, sexy and sensitive?

Looked like she just found a new type.

THE FOLLOWING MORNING Aria returned to the scene of Chloe's murder with Selena and Blanca. The white shepherd sensed it was time to work, and her restlessness permeated the car. Aria bounced her leg in response to the tension, but Selena seemed unfazed. If both dog and handler were excited, they'd be pinging off the interior of the car and Blanca probably wouldn't be able to work.

They had the shirt Chloe had been wearing the night of her murder. Selena would let Blanca sniff it, and see if she could track Chloe's progress on that road. With any luck, Chloe's scent would lead them to the endpoint of that tunnel and the drug storage area.

Aria parked on the road above the gravel path next to the water. She led the way down the trail, with Selena keeping Blanca on a tight leash behind her. The scrap of yellow crime scene tape, still stuck to a bush, waved at them.

Blanca whined and her ears perked up as Selena told her to sit, using the German word. Selena pulled Chloe's top from the bag and held it to Blanca's nose, which twitched and quivered.

Selena then unclipped Blanca's leash and said, *"Track."*

Blanca put her snout in the air and sniffed. She trotted a few steps forward and then dropped her nose to the ground and snuffled along the gravel. The dog alternated between sniffing the air and the ground. When she reached the dark stain, somewhat diluted by the recent rain, where Chloe had lost her life, Blanca sat and barked sharply two times.

"Good dog." Selena stood in front of Blanca and offered her the shirt again. She pointed in the other direction. *"Keep going. Track!"*

Blanca followed her path back to where they started and kept going in the other direction.

Every time the K-9 paused, Aria would hold her breath as Selena shouted more commands.

As the marshy ground got more uneven, Blanca began veering toward the water's edge.

Aria whispered to Selena, "Will it be harder for her to track the scent in the soft reeds as opposed to the ground?"

"That rain didn't help, but she should be okay—if there's anything there."

Finally, Blanca made a decision and sat next to a pile of muck, barking twice.

"She may have found something." Selena hustled toward her dog. *"Good dog."*

Before Selena reached Blanca, the K-9 was on the move again, pacing and circling the area by the water. Occasionally, she'd stop and sit and give out two barks, which Selena had explained was her "alert" signal, telling them she'd noticed something.

Aria said, "She seems to like that spot."

"But she can't seem to alert to just one." Selena gave a sharp whistle between her teeth and ordered Blanca out with an *"out"* command.

Blanca retreated and returned to her handler's side, tongue lolling out of the side of her mouth. Selena withdrew a bottle of water and tipped it. Blanca lapped at the stream of water.

Selena pointed to the spot. "Do you want to have a look?"

Aria didn't have to be asked twice. She slogged through the reeds and wet grasses toward the water seeping onto the land. "This place would make perfect sense for the endpoint of a tunnel under the lake."

She scanned the space, kicking at rises with the toe of her shoe, getting on her knees and scrabbling against the dirt with her fingers.

Selena called out to her. "Let the CSI team have a crack at it. We'll make our report to Alana and Max."

Aria waded out of the mire, pulling her sneakers from the glop beneath her feet, brushing the wet knees of her jeans. "Hey, do we know if Chloe had grass and mud stuck to her boots? That might tell us something."

"Unless she cleaned them off." Selena leashed Blanca again and patted her head. "I hope this is it."

"Blanca could be our hero." Ara knew enough from the police academy and the K-9 units at Detroit PD to understand that she couldn't wrap her arms around Blanca and bury her face in the dog's thick fur. So instead, she said, *"Good dog."*

They returned to the car, and Selena called Alana to tell her about Blanca's alerts and to send Max and a CSI team from the PHPD.

When she ended the call, she pulled a pack of hand sanitizer wipes from her bag and held it out to Aria. "We might as well eat lunch while we're waiting."

"Is Blanca going to go back to the scene?" Aria plucked a wipe from the package and cleaned off her hands. Nothing much she could do for her jeans.

"No, we'll stay behind when CSI gets here. I don't want her to get confused with all the different scents." Selena tugged a plastic bag from her backpack and plunged her hand inside. "Did you get a ham on rye, too?"

"Pastrami."

Selena handed her one of the wrapped sandwiches they'd picked up on the way in case Blanca kept them out here all day.

"Napkins?" Aria held out her hand and Selena slapped a handful into her palm.

She dangled a bag of chips from her fingertips for a second, reading the print, and then tossed them into Aria's lap. "Pastrami and jalapeño chips. I hope you're not meeting Grayson Rhodes after this."

Aria had been in the process of ripping open her bag of chips. Her hands jerked and the chips spilled all over her napkin-covered lap. "What does that mean?"

"It means your breath is going to be…spicy." Selena carefully unwrapped her ham sandwich.

"And why should I care if Grayson Rhodes thinks I have…spicy breath?" Aria collected the chips and dropped them back into the bag, popping one into her mouth.

"He's a good-looking guy, and you're spending a lot of time with him." Selena waved her sandwich at Aria. "Not that I'm saying it's not all legit."

Selena bit into her sandwich and then wiped her mouth.

"Alana's the one who sent me with him to visit his nephew last night."

"What's up with her, anyway? Although, I shouldn't be asking the new kid on the block." Selena shook out a little packet of mustard. "But take it from me, Alana hasn't been her usual energetic self."

"Even I noticed she's looking tired—doesn't stop her from working ten times harder than the rest of us, though." Aria wiped the spicy jalapeño seasoning on the napkin in her lap. "I swear she had tears in her eyes yesterday."

"Maybe the work just gets to her sometimes. Nice to know she's human like the rest of us."

Aria nodded and took a big bite of her sandwich, just happy the subject of the conversation had switched from her and Grayson to Alana.

"How *did* it go with the baby last night?"

Aria dabbed her lips. Grayson hadn't wanted her to tell anyone about his room getting tossed. "It went well. Little Danny obviously remembered his uncle, and Grayson was impressed with the foster parents, who are right out of the guide for foster parents."

"Here they come." Selena adjusted her rearview mirror, Blanca stirring in the back. "Don't you worry, girl. Your work is done for the day, and I'll give you a big meal."

"Selena, you and Blanca don't have to wait for me. Once you tell Alana what happened with Blanca, you can take off. I'll get a ride back with someone else."

"Sounds good."

They finished off their lunches in a hurry and then took Alana and Max down to the water's edge where Selena explained what had happened with Blanca.

When Selena left, Aria stood with Alana as Max and the CSI team searched the area, digging, collecting, thrashing through the reeds.

After more than an hour, Max popped up and shook his head. Aria's stomach dropped. "Nothing? There has to be something there. Why would Chloe be near the water's edge?"

"Maybe she took a boat to this spot." Alana kicked a small rock and it skipped and bounced on the ground. "Damn. I thought this was it. You and Axel are going to have to have another go at Tony Balducci. Really put the screws to him this time. The kid's not too bright. Use that."

Alana waved her arm in the air and called out to Max, "Keep it up for a while longer to make sure you're not missing anything. I'm going back." She spun around and made a beeline for the trail leading up to the main road.

"Alana." Aria had to jog to keep up with the director. "Can you give me a ride back to the station? I'm going to try to get together with Axel to plot out our next move against Tony."

Without turning around, Alana called over her shoulder, "Sure."

Aria scrambled up the path in Alana's wake, and they both climbed into her rental car. The director sat behind the wheel, her finger resting on the ignition button.

Snapping her seat belt, Aria glanced at Alana's frozen profile. "Um, where's Amanda? I haven't seen her around."

"She's spending a lot of time in the war room. I couldn't function without her, especially—" Alana broke off and clutched the steering wheel with both hands, resting her forehead on the top.

Aria's breath hitched in her throat, wishing one of the other team members was there instead of her. She reached out tentatively and put her hand on Alana's arm. "Do you want to tell me what's wrong, Alana?"

With her head still on the steering wheel, Alana turned to her and Aria's heart jumped as the director's professional mask slipped away. Her dark eyes shimmered with tears and her mouth trembled.

"Alana, what's wrong?"

Alana lifted her head and took a deep, shuddering breath. "It's this Blah Boatie case."

"Th-the dead women? The baby?" Aria's mind sifted

through the cases the TCD handled with Alana at the helm—child trafficking, kidnapping, serial murders, bombings—Alana had seen it all.

"When I was eighteen, before I enlisted in the Army, I had a baby, a daughter." Alana gazed into space and time through the windshield. "My father was old school, a colonel in the Army. I gave the baby up for adoption."

"I'm sorry. I didn't know."

"Nobody knows, except my husband." Alana blinked. "It was an open adoption, and I always figured my daughter would get curious and find me. She never did. But I found her, and I followed her life from afar. When Miko became addicted to opioids, I knew about that, too."

Aria covered her mouth with her hand. "I'm so sorry. No wonder this case is getting under your skin."

"I wanted to step in, help her, make her better, like I'm sure Grayson Rhodes wanted to do with his sister, but you can't make a user stop using. Ask your Mr. Rhodes about that."

Aria let the implication pass and retrieved a tissue from her bag. She handed it to Alana, who crushed it in her fist.

"I'm assuming Miko's adoptive parents know about her addiction. Have they tried to intervene? Maybe under the circumstances, it's time for you to step forward."

Alana lifted one shoulder and the corner of her mouth twitched. "It's too late for all that. Miko died of an overdose six years ago."

Chapter Fifteen

Aria clutched the base of her throat with one hand, her pulse thudding beneath her fingertips. "I'm sorry."

The words sounded small and inadequate. No wonder Alana had been on edge. Every time she saw one of those dead blah boaties, misguided, lost, opioids in their systems, she must've been thinking about her own daughter.

Alana continued, almost as if Aria wasn't beside her in the car. "The day I found out she died, I'd been working a kidnapping case, helping other families find their children when I'd just lost my only daughter forever. I attended her funeral—a stranger in the back, on the outside, an observer, just as I'd been her entire life."

Aria kept her lips sealed under Alana's need to unburden herself. Another "sorry" wasn't going to ease this woman's pain.

Her eyes dry now, Alana shredded the tissue in her lap. "At the funeral, I watched Miko's parents—they'd named her Tania—bent, broken, their faces ravaged by grief. I felt the same way inside, beneath the clenched jaw, the rigid muscles. I wanted to scream and cry and beat my breast for the world to see, but I'd given up that right."

Aria clasped Alana's hand. "You were still her mother. You had every right…and you still do."

"Maybe I should've stepped forward, inserted myself into her life. Maybe I could've gotten her to turn her life around. Or maybe I was the reason she started using in the first place."

"Stop." Aria smacked her hand against the dashboard. "You, of all people, with the work we do, understand that nobody can make an addict stop using. And thousands of children are adopted every year. It isn't a precursor for addiction."

"I know that. You're right." Alana pressed the mangled tissue to her nose. "You're so vehement, so passionate. No wonder Grayson Rhodes turns to you."

Aria's mouth dropped open as she struggled to find the words to respond.

But then Alana squared her shoulders, pinning them back against the seat, and punched the starter on the car with her knuckle. "Let's get back to work. We have a drug dealer to catch. And please don't bring this up to anyone else on the team. Nobody needs to know my personal weaknesses. I'm sorry I dumped this on you. I'll be fine."

"Of course." Aria folded her hands in her lap.

Talk about personal weaknesses. She was falling for someone intricately tied to her first case on the Tactical Crime Division…and everyone knew it.

ARIA SPENT THE rest of the afternoon in the TCD's war room at the PHPD, reviewing the underwater photos Max had taken of the tunnel entrance and meeting up with Axel to review their strategy for questioning Tony the next day.

A few surreptitious glances at Alana assured Aria that the director had bounced back with a vengeance after her confession in the car. She was all business as she dictated to Amanda and jetted between Max and Opaline, comparing the maps to the photos, and Selena reviewing the area where Blanca had alerted. Was she regretting it now?

Aria felt honored that Alana trusted her with her confidence, but she didn't have a choice. The story probably never would've come out if Aria hadn't hit up Alana for a ride. She'd caught the director in a weak moment, but if Alana feared the revelation about her daughter and her death from opioids would tarnish her authority, she had nothing to worry about. Alana's disclosure had only solidified Aria's respect for the woman, and made Aria feel as if she could trust her boss with anything.

Axel took a seat across from her, straddling it and crossing his arms over the back. "You look tired. We're all good on our technique for interrogating Balducci tomorrow, so why don't you head back to the hotel, get something to eat and relax."

"When everyone's still here, working?"

"Nobody will think that. You've more than pulled your load on this case." He cranked his head back and forth. "Besides, look around. Carly's not here, and I'd bet she'd like some company for dinner. You two can even work through dinner, if you insist. I know she has some results for the drugs the women were carrying, and she'd probably like to run those by you."

Stretching her arms over her head, Aria yawned and said, "You convinced me."

"Good, bright and early tomorrow morning, then. We're going to nail Balducci to the wall."

Aria approached Alana, hovering over Amanda as she entered text in a spreadsheet, and touched her shoulder. "I'm going back to the hotel. I'm going to see if Carly has some info on those drugs."

Alana twisted her head over her shoulder and smiled. "You do that. Get a little rest while you're at it."

Aria hesitated, raising her eyebrows. Alana straightened to her full height, which was a few inches shorter than Aria's, and took her by the shoulders. She lowered her voice. "I'm fine. Thanks for listening, but there's nothing for you to worry about. Nothing."

Aria smiled and gave Alana a quick, one-armed hug—and didn't care what any of the team members thought about her gesture.

Blinking back tears, Aria left the conference room and took one of the rental cars back to the hotel. If Carly wanted to discuss her findings with Aria, it must not be that urgent because she hadn't answered her texts. Axel had probably just wanted to give her an excuse to leave.

And no wonder—Aria leaned in close to the full-length mirror on the hotel closet's door and ran her fingers through her messy hair. The damp spots on her knees from searching the swampy area next to the lake today had dried into dirty, stiff stains.

When she'd joined the team for the first time several days ago, which now seemed like a lifetime ago, she'd been worried about a ponytail. Now, look at her.

She called room service to order some soup and then hopped in the shower. By the time she'd changed into some sweats and dragged out her FBI binder on interrogations, her food arrived.

She slurped her soup from a spoon as she flipped through the pages of the binder, reading transcripts of interrogations—some of which had been conducted by Axel Morrow. She'd follow his lead tomorrow, and hopefully they could trap Tony into revealing the head honcho. He had to know something. He'd been the hit man. The guy at the top had to have some level of trust in him.

The presence of Danny had unraveled Tony. In addition to Tony's DNA on that tissue she'd found at the murder scene, Danny's DNA was also present. Tony had used his own tissue to wipe Danny's nose or tears. Danny had led them to his mother's killer.

Aria pushed the binder off her lap to grab her buzzing phone. Selena had sent a text, along with a picture of Blanca, thanking her for coming out today with her and her K-9. Aria replied with a smiling doggie face.

Blanca had been circling the same area by the water but hadn't taken them any farther. Could Chloe have come from the water? No boat was found, but Tony could've taken care of that. Maybe the tunnel had been in a different area.

Checking the time on her phone, Aria scooted off the bed and grabbed her grimy jeans from the top of her suitcase. She still had the keys to one of the rental cars and a flashlight. It couldn't hurt to take a quick trip back out there, not that she believed she'd find the tunnel entrance, but she was restless anyway.

She pulled on her jeans and layered a few shirts under her jacket before stuffing her feet into a pair of sneakers. She crept down the hallway, not wanting to raise an alarm and convince her teammates she'd lost her mind.

Ten minutes later, she pulled onto the side of the road above the lake access and exited the car, flashlight in hand. She followed the beam down the path to the gravel road that snaked beside the lake.

She located the place where Blanca had alerted, marked by the trampled grasses and slashed bushes. She slogged into the marshy soil, sweeping aside the long reeds with her arms, like a windmill.

The rain had never materialized today and the wind blew just enough to lift the ends of her hair from her shoulders, so the faint sound of splashing water had her freezing in place, her feet sinking into the muck.

She hunched over as the sound grew louder—plop, splash, plop, splash. She pulled her gun from the pocket of her jacket and killed her light.

A dark shape appeared on the water and her muscles twitched as it drew closer. A man's body rocked back and forth, the oars in his hands dipping in the water and sluicing it back, propelling him closer and closer to the shore…and her hiding place.

Several feet away, he pulled the boat onto the shore, securing it. As he unfolded to his full height, the hood of his sweatshirt fell back and the moonlight caught the gleaming strands of his blond hair.

She gasped and loosened her hold on her weapon. "Grayson?"

His head jerked toward her as his hand dipped into his pocket, where she knew he had his Glock. "Who's there?"

"It's Aria." She turned on her flashlight and held the beam to her face.

"I was ready to shoot you."

"Great." She slipped her SIG-Sauer into her pocket. "What are you doing out here?"

"This isn't my first time." He kicked the boat with the toe of his boot and trudged over the grass to stand beside her. "I figured since you didn't text me, you didn't find anything today with the K-9."

"Yeah, well, the dog alerted, but nothing turned up." It had taken a lot of willpower for her to resist contacting him today. "How'd it go at work today after the break-in last night? No more trouble?"

"I pretended nothing happened. When I told the motel manager about the door, I said a drunken friend had kicked it in and I didn't want to report it to the police. He was cool with that. Nobody knew about it at work, and nobody was acting suspiciously. If someone there does know my true identity or suspects me of being a plant, he's not saying."

"But somebody knows something, or your motel room wouldn't have been targeted." She rubbed her hands against the thighs of her jeans, suddenly cold.

"You should have some gloves." He took her arm. "At least get out of this muck."

She stamped her feet when they hit the gravel.

Grayson cocked his head. "If you didn't find anything out here, what are you doing? And why are you by yourself?"

The reproachful tone in his voice had her grinding her teeth. "I'm a special agent with the FBI. I don't need an escort. I don't need a bodyguard and, unlike Danny, I don't need a nanny."

"Whoa." He held up his hands. "I hit a nerve. I'm sorry."

She flipped her hair over her shoulder. "Sometimes I think you forget who I am. I know I haven't acted in the most professional manner on this case…"

"I think you're a kickass FBI agent. You're smart, fearless and professional when it matters." He caught her hand. "But you're right. I forget because I'm falling hard for you, Aria. Hard and fast. I know myself. I don't usually do this. I'm careful, especially with my heart. You're different. Special. I don't want this to end…"

She dropped her lashes because, if she met his eyes, she'd invite his kisses again. "I—I don't know what to say, Grayson."

"You don't have to say anything at all." He squeezed her hand and released it. "I just lost my sister. You're right. My behavior toward you is over the top and unreasonable, but I can't handle another loss. This thing you do…terrifies me."

She flexed and then curled her fingers, missing his touch already. He'd told her in the space of a minute he was falling in love with her but couldn't handle her job. They couldn't be together. She always knew that.

She brushed her hand against his, selfishly craving the comfort of his arms.

His fingers tangled with hers and he ducked his head toward her.

Then a shot rang out in the night and Aria dropped to the ground.

Chapter Sixteen

Grayson's body jerked at the loud report and a soft whizzing sound behind his head.

At his feet, Aria wrapped her arms around his legs and hissed. "Get down. Someone just took a shot at us."

Grayson dove to the ground next to her at the same time another crack split the air above him. The damp earth absorbed his fall as he frantically scrambled for the gun in his pocket. "Did you see where it came from?"

Aria, crouching behind a bush, clutching her 9mm, held a finger to her lips. She whispered. "Must have come from the road above."

Rising to his knees, Grayson turned toward the road but Aria kicked out her leg, her shoe landing against his thigh.

"Keep low and still. The shooter has the advantage. You're never going to get a shot at him from down here. He'll kill you on your way up." Her voice caught in her throat. "Call 9-1-1."

Grayson fished his phone from his pocket. "We can't just be sitting ducks."

"We're not. We have cover where we are now—as long as you stay down. Keep your head below the reeds, and he won't be able to see you." She swung her gun in front of her. "If he tries to come down that path to get a better shot, we have the advantage."

"We have the jump on him if he tries to come by water, too." Grayson nodded at his boat, its prow wedged against the shore. He called 9-1-1 from his cell and referenced the sight of Chloe Larsen's murder. "Anyone else?"

With her gaze pinned to the path leading to the road, she reached into her pocket and tossed her phone to him. "Call my director, Alana Suzuki. She's listed as TCD on my phone."

Grayson made the call. A woman answered after the second ring. Didn't these people ever sleep?

"Suzuki."

"Director Suzuki, this is Grayson Rhodes, Chloe Larsen's broth—" He barely finished his intro as she spoke over his last word.

"Is Aria all right?"

"Aria's fine, but we're under fire at the site of my sister's murder. We're by the lake, and someone's taking shots at us from the road. We already called 9-1-1, and Aria asked me to call you, too."

The director sighed on the other end of the line. "You'll be fine with Aria, and the PHPD first responders will scare away the shooter. Tell her I'm on my way."

She ended the call and Grayson was left with his mouth hanging open. Director Suzuki had been worried about Aria at first because he'd been the one to make the call, but then she'd flipped the script and told him *he'd* be safe with Aria.

Since the shots were first fired, Grayson had felt the weight of taking care of and protecting Aria, but she'd been the one in control of the situation. Even realizing a bullet had just whizzed by his head, he'd been too shocked to drop to the ground. And then he'd added dumb to dumber by thinking he could get into a shootout with a gunman with a vantage point.

"What did she say?"

"She's on the way." He put Aria's phone in his pocket. He didn't want to distract her in case the gunman came at them. Grayson needed her professionalism now to get them out of this mess.

His heart pounded as he watched the water for movement. When the first wail of the sirens reached his ears, he blew out a breath. "They're on the way."

"Just keep down until they get here with the lights and sirens and weapons. The shooter could still be in the area."

Two minutes later, the scene was awash with cops, lights and voices. Grayson waited for Aria to make the first move. She holstered her gun and signaled him to do the same. Then she rose slowly with her hands in the air, her badge pinched between her fingers.

She shouted, "FBI. We're the ones who made the call."

Grayson followed suit, rising from the muck as if being reborn, raising his hands.

The first cop on the scene swept his light across their faces. "I know, Special Agent Calletti. What happened out here?"

As the cops canvassed the area and looked for the two bullets that had missed, Grayson and Aria spoke to a sergeant. Aria did the talking. She had the expertise to describe what had happened, and the sergeant didn't even blink when she explained what Grayson had been doing there.

A dog barked and as Grayson followed the sound to the path leading to the lakeside road, he spied several of Aria's teammates with the director in the lead. He hoped she wasn't going to be reprimanded for being here…with him.

When the PHPD sergeant finished his questioning, Director Suzuki approached them. "I suppose you didn't get a look at the shooter?"

"Not at all." Aria shook her head. "I think he was hiding on the road. Any shell casings recovered?"

"No. No evidence at all up there."

"We must be onto something. Blanca wasn't wrong. The drug organization doesn't want anyone snooping around this area."

"Or they were after him." The director leveled a finger at Grayson. "They probably know your relationship to Chloe, and they know you're not some random dockworker. Did you two come together?"

"No." Aria jerked her thumb over her shoulder. "Mr. Rhodes paddled here by boat—and it's not the first time, he told me. I just couldn't relax. I kept thinking about Blanca today, and thought I'd have another look. We just…ran into each other."

"That's good." Director Suzuki rubbed her gloved hands together. "At least nobody followed the two of you together. Even if they know he's Chloe's brother, they still might think that Mr. Rhodes is a grieving family member returning to the sight of his sister's murder, and is not working with the FBI, but someone obviously thinks you're getting too close or too nosy."

"Technically, I'm not working with the FBI, ma'am. I'm happy to give you information when I hear it, but it's not like I'm on the payroll. I'm going to continue showing up on the docks. I don't believe anyone there knows my true purpose—even the supervisor who was ordered to hire me with no questions asked doesn't know why."

"The good news is, the shooter didn't kill you…or Aria."

Grayson chuckled despite the gravity of the situation. "Yeah, I'd say that's good news for both of us."

Aria tapped her chin. "What Alana means is maybe the gunman didn't intend to kill us, just warn us off."

"That had the opposite effect." Grayson swept his arm to the side to encompass the lights and activity.

Almost an hour later, the search started to wind down. The shooter hadn't left behind any evidence, but Aria's Tactical Crime Division decided to search the area again tomorrow.

Grayson pulled Aria aside and put his lips close to her ear. "Thanks for saving my life tonight."

Her dark eyes widened. "Do you mean because the bullet missed you as you bent down to kiss me?"

"I guess that shot would've come a lot closer if I hadn't had the sudden urge to kiss you." His lips twisted into a smile. "But that's not what I meant."

"No?"

"Under fire, I had no clue what to do, even with a gun in my hand. I could've put us both at risk." He rubbed his chin. "You didn't need my protection, did you?"

"In that instance, no, I didn't." She broke their eye contact by leaning to brush off her filthy jeans. "I'm not your sister, Grayson."

"You made that abundantly clear…and I'm not your father."

Still bent over, she turned her head and looked at him, her eyes deep and unfathomable. "These jeans are hopeless, aren't they?"

"About as bad as mine." He pointed up to the place where someone had just been shooting at them. "Can I walk you back to your car, or are you going to stick around and wrap this up?"

"I think I can leave." She waved one hand over her head. "Alana, I'm heading back."

He followed her up the path to the road, now flooded with cars and a news van. "Are they blocking you in?"

"I don't think so." She strode to her car and tripped to a stop. "Looks like the cops missed this."

Grayson whistled and kicked her slashed tire. "Guess you're not going anywhere, unless you want to hop in my boat."

"Not a good idea." Her gaze flicked to her teammates still working below. "I can get a ride back by land."

"Then I'm going to hit the road…um, the water. I have a full day of work ahead of me tomorrow."

As he turned, Aria called after him. "Be careful. Someone knows who you are."

"I know who *you* are, Aria Calletti." He kept walking, his sodden boots crunching the gravel as he started down the path to the lake.

And he wanted her now more than ever.

ARIA FLICKED THE loose hair from her eyes and brushed on some black mascara with a heavy hand. She was still Tony's friend, someone he could trust. She was the Italian girl next door, not the hardcore FBI agent interrogating a criminal.

She added a little lipstick and smacked her lips together. Maybe that almost-kiss had saved Grayson's life last night. What had he meant when he'd said he knew her? What had he meant when he'd said he was falling in love with her?

She sighed, dropped her lipstick into her makeup bag and stuffed the bag into her purse. Time to shift her focus to Tony and the interrogation. She'd finally heard back from Carly through a text, and though they'd tracked down the kind of drugs on Chloe, it hadn't yielded as much information as she'd hoped. At least, nothing to help them with questioning Tony more.

Axel tapped on the bathroom door. "You ready to roll?"

"All done." She pushed open the door and patted her face. "Did I overdo it?"

"Not at all. You look like a woman Tony might hit up at The Tavern."

"Thanks." She fluffed up the ends of her hair. "I think."

They entered the interrogation room together, and Tony sat straighter in his chair, his smile a little less cocky, his chest a little less puffed up. "Are you gonna move me out of here soon?"

Aria perched on the edge of her chair, while Axel swung out a chair and sat, facing Tony across the metal table secured to the floor, just like Tony's chair. "You like it here, huh? Safer than prison, for sure."

"If anyone thinks I talked, I'm in trouble. But I didn't tell you nothing you didn't already know, right? You knew I killed them girls." Tony licked his lips. "Right? One of the other prisoners here told me cops sometimes lie just to get you to say things."

"We know you killed those women." Axel patted the thick folder at his elbow. "We know they were smuggling drugs. We just need to know who they were working for. Who you were working for."

Tony's gaze darted from Axel's face to Aria's. "I—I don't really know that."

Aria leaned forward, her elbow planted on the table, her chin in her palm. "C'mon, Tony. We don't want his full name, address, marital status and social security number. We just need something—even talk on the street. Anyone ever meet him? Have a beef with him? Everyone bitches about the boss, right, Axel?"

Axel smirked. "I know you do."

Tony's head tilted to the right and his gaze dropped to the V-neck of Aria's red sweater. "Yeah, there was some talk."

"And what was the word on the street?" Axel tapped his pen on the folder. "Cross him and you're dead? I mean, that's what happened to the blah boaties, right?

They went into a little business on the side, the boss found out and ordered the hits."

"That's why I'm not saying nothing." Tony crossed his arms. "I confessed to killing those bitches, and that's it."

Aria slid one hand beneath her thigh to stop herself from slapping Tony's face. Instead she smiled. "But your boss doesn't know that. We haven't released any information about your arrest. As far as your boss knows, you're in here singin' like a freakin' bird."

"And that's—" Axel drilled his finger into the tabletop "—what we're gonna put out there. Furthermore, if you don't start coughing up some information, we'll ship you off to prison with absolutely no protection."

Tony's Adam's apple bobbed and a bead of sweat formed on his brow. "What kind of protection can I get?"

"We can do whatever we want." Axel swept a hand in the air. "We can give you what amounts to witness protection in the prison—different name, anonymity for your specific crimes, maybe even a few creature comforts."

Aria held her breath. So far, they'd managed Tony without any lawyers present. She was impressed with how far Axel could take him without his insisting on legal representation, but Tony trusted them now.

Tony slicked back his hair. "Can we start with a haircut? And maybe something besides these slippers on my feet? My feet are always cold, man."

Not as cold as those women. Aria ground her teeth

together but managed to squeeze out a few words. "I think those things can be arranged. Axel?"

"We can iron out those details…when you start talking. All we've heard from you so far is 'I don't know, I don't know,' and *we* know that's BS, Tony. What's the word on the street about the guy at the top?"

Tony dropped his chin to his chest and watched his fidgeting fingers. "Lives in Port Huron—at least, right now. Been running the ring for a few years, always using different girls to run the cruise to Canada, different girls but the same—you know, blah boaties."

Aria swallowed and relaxed her tense muscles. "Does he swap out the girls by killing them and finding new ones?"

Tony's head shot up. "Nah. I mean I don't think so. These girls were skimming something off the top—a little Apache for themselves or money."

Aria said quietly, "Brandy wasn't."

"What do you mean?" Tony's body stiffened and he gripped the edge of the table.

They'd kept Brandy's murder from Tony on purpose. Now seemed the right time to drop the news.

"Aww, you didn't know about that, Tony?" Axel tipped his chair onto the back legs, folding his hands behind his head. "Someone killed Brandy—strangled her and threw her over the side of a boat—*the* boat, *Fun Times*."

Tony swore and buried his head in his folded arms on the table. With a muffled voice, he said, "I told her to keep quiet and calm down. They must've known she was getting nervous, close to talking."

Close to talking to Grayson. Is that why someone took a shot at him last night?

"Seems to me this kingpin is ruthless—punishes his enemies. You can help us get him off the street. Protect yourself, Tony."

The chain on the table jingled as Tony bounced his knee up and down. He raised his head, his eyes bright with tears over Brandy.

Aria reached out and laid a hand on his arm. "Think about Brandy, Tony. Think about your friend. Think about that baby, the same age as your niece. What would your niece do if she lost her mother?"

Tony swiped a hand across his nose. "I don't know his full name…like you said. It's just an initial."

Aria exchanged a glance with Axel. It was better than nothing.

She increased the pressure on Tony's arm. "What initial?"

"V."

Axel let his chair drop forward with a bang and hunched over the table. "V? Just V? That's all you got? I don't know if that's enough for fuzzy slippers. What do you think, Aria?"

Tony's arm vibrated beneath her touch and she withdrew her hand. "What do you think the V stands for? First name? Last name?"

"Not sure." Tony glanced at her but his gaze kept sliding back to Axel, now looming in front of him and seemingly not going anywhere.

"Let's play a game." Axel pulled back and steepled

his fingers, tapping them together. "What do you think V could stand for? Aria, you go."

She lifted her shoulders. "Vincent, Victor, Vance, Vernon."

"Your turn, Tony." Axel banged his fist on the metal table.

Tony jumped. "I dunno. Victoria, Vanessa, Veronica, Vivian…"

Tony trailed off, his face blanching as Axel propped his chin on top of his now clasped hands and whispered. "The drug kingpin is a woman."

Chapter Seventeen

"A woman with a first, last or nickname that starts with *V*." Alana gave a nod to Max as the whole team crowded into the war room. "Max has been cultivating some local informants since we arrived. The drug scene is alive and well in Port Huron."

Aria studied Alana's face as she stood at the front of the room. Confession must've been good for Alana's soul because the pep was back in her step, the verve back in her voice. Aria wasn't taking any credit for the director getting back on firm footing on this case. She'd just been in the right place at the right time for Alana to spill her guts. Maybe she'd take a little credit. Alana may have felt more comfortable revealing her secret to Aria, the newest agent. Everyone had secrets.

Carly held up a small, plastic bag containing two blue pills and shook it in the air. "With Aria's help, we've identified the fentanyl the blah boaties were carrying as Blue Apache. That's its street name here, and any junkie worth his or her salt knows where to score Blue Apache."

Including the guys on the docks. The stuff was all

over the place, and it would be hard to trace any particular lot. Aria stroked the phone in her pocket. After the interview with Tony and the explosive information she and Axel had extracted from him, Alana had called an emergency meeting at the station and herded them all in here.

Alana and the team hadn't wanted to use Grayson as an official informant for a variety of reasons, including his safety, but Aria knew Grayson had no immediate plans to step away from his undercover job at the docks. Why not make use of that? The man could more than take care of himself. The good news was that he'd finally realized last night that he didn't have to take care of her, too. Aria hadn't had one second to text the news to Grayson—but she had every intention of doing so.

And what had she realized? She cared for him. The thought of leaving him behind after this case was over hurt and distracted her.

"…and Aria."

Feeling several pairs of eyes drilling into her, Aria jerked her head up. "I'm sorry. What?"

"I said—" Alana shot her a stern look from the head of the table "—you will stand by with Axel in case Max and Carly turn up any information on V. The two of you can move on it right away."

"Yes, ma'am." A few of the team members snickered. "Uh, Alana."

Alana's lips twitched. "After the shots fired at Aria and… Mr. Rhodes last night. Selena and Blanca are at the first murder sight today to see if there are any similarities in the layout of the land. Anything else?"

Rihanna raised a finger with a perfectly polished fingernail at the tip. "You may have seen the news. Tony Balducci's name has been released as a suspect in the murder of the three women. So far, there is no connection to the drug trade, and we want to keep it that way. If Carly and Max are going out looking for this V, we don't want her to take flight."

"I also have something." Opaline flicked her purple-edged locks out of her face. "I've been working with Customs on the Canadian side of the river, and they have records of the *Fun Times* cruises. They're working now to get the passenger names. Those are most likely our dealers in Canada."

Alana brought her hands together. "Good work, people. We just need to bring in V, so she doesn't set up shop in some other unsuspecting border community."

"I have a question." Max scooted up to the table. "Do we know for a fact that a hit was put out on those women because they were skimming money or drugs? Or was that V taking care of business before she packed up and moved somewhere else?"

Axel answered. "We don't know for sure. That's what Balducci told us."

Amanda popped her head up from behind her computer screen. "If she were doing cleanup, that's hardly a ringing endorsement for the next set of employees."

"If the next batch of blah boaties even hears about it or connects the dots…" Aria shrugged. "As long as there are addicts, V will have an endless supply of employees."

Biting her bottom lip, Aria slid a gaze to Alana's impassive face.

"Aria's not wrong about that." Alana clapped her hands. "Let's get on this. I'm ready to wrap this up and leave Port Huron—no disrespect to PH."

As Axel rose, Aria tugged on his sleeve. "I'll be here at the station if you need me. I'm going to grab some lunch and have a look at any photos coming from Selena of the first murder sight."

"Good to know. I'll be in and out." He held out his fist for a bump. "Great job in that interview room, Aria. Balducci had no intention of revealing V's moniker… until he did."

"Learning from the master."

Axel lifted one shoulder, too humble to acknowledge the truth, and followed Max out the door.

As the only other person left in the room, Amanda glanced up from finishing her notes. "Never got your birthday, Aria."

"June 3."

Amanda tapped on her keyboard. "Makes you a Gemini—two personalities. I guess you're in the right job for that."

"You're right. I think I do have two personalities." One the professional and one falling hopelessly in love with Grayson Rhodes.

GRAYSON CUPPED HIS phone in his hand and read the text from Aria on his way to the lunch truck. The person at the head of this drug organization, the person who'd ordered his sister's death, was a woman. Damn.

As he waited for his lunch, he texted Aria that he'd call her in a few minutes. After he picked up his greasy burger from the truck's window and squirted ketchup on his equally greasy fries, Grayson carried his lunch to the end of the docks, where the FBI had been diving for those tunnels. As he usually ate lunch alone, nobody questioned him—too busy talking about Tony's arrest.

He straddled one of the wooden stumps left there for some unknown reason and called Aria.

She answered breathlessly as if she'd just run a 10K. "Can you talk?"

"I'm eating lunch by myself. Are you all right after last night?" He snapped his mouth shut. He shouldn't be asking her questions like that.

Her low voice caressed his ear. "I'm fine. Are you all right? I'm so glad you were there last night. Two is better than one."

Grayson got so excited, he almost dropped his phone in the ketchup. "Yeah, we made a good team. The drug kingpin is a woman, huh?"

"Kind of sickening when you think about how she's putting young women at risk."

"Well, I wouldn't exactly hold her up as a role model for young women." He popped two fries into his mouth. "What do you need from me?"

"You don't have to do anything, Grayson. Two of my team members are out there right now, leaning on PHPD informants for information about this V and the fentanyl she sells. Something will turn up. I know from experience, drug dealers don't work in a vacuum. Tony had heard the name V and others may know more than just the nickname."

"I know I don't *have* to do anything, Aria, but I'm still working at the docks. Nobody is the wiser where I'm concerned. Nobody knows I fingered Tony Balducci. I'm still just the new guy. Maybe they're a little freer in their conversation around me because I don't know the lay of the land. Whoever shot at me—at us—last night is not connected to the docks. Whoever broke into my place is not connected to the docks."

"But if V targeted you, she might have contacts at the dock. She'd warn those contacts about you."

Grayson squinted at his coworkers eating their lunch, the younger ones horsing around, the older ones bone-weary and busy shoveling food into their mouths. "Hasn't happened yet. Hey, I have some good news."

"Would love to hear it."

"My assistant, Patrick, has started the hunt for a nanny. He's going to use a service he and his partner used. They do all the vetting and they will send over the ones that meet my criteria. All I need to do is interview them."

"That's fantastic news. I'm sure you'll find someone perfect for Danny."

"I have a favor to ask." Grayson held his breath.

"Anything. After all the help you've given us, putting yourself in danger, we can't make you an honorary FBI agent, but we'll do whatever we can to assist you."

"I don't want everyone's help…just yours. Can you be there when I interview for nannies?"

"I…" She sniffed, cleared her throat and coughed. "Are you sure? None of my siblings has a nanny."

"Yeah, because they use you. Because of all your nieces and nephews, you have a better idea of what babies need and want, and the important qualities for a good caregiver." He curled his hand around the phone. "I'd really appreciate your help. You know, obviously when this case is all over and you have some time."

"I'd be happy to help, if I can swing it timewise."

"You've taken a big weight off my shoulders. Patrick will be glad to hear I have someone else involved in the decision-making process, too." A distant whistle blew and Grayson shifted his gaze to the work area. "Lunchtime is over. I'll see what I can find out about V."

He cut off the call before Aria could protest. He dumped his unfinished lunch into a bag and tossed it in a garbage can.

When he returned to work, Grayson managed to grab a pallet alongside Chuck and linger as the older man stopped to rest.

Grayson nudged Chuck's shoulder. "I forgot to ask you earlier, Chuck, how's your sister taking the news about Tony?"

"As you'd expect. Hit her hard. I think she's been at church ever since she found out." Chuck rubbed the back of his neck. "I just don't get it. Maybe there's some mistake."

"Did he know any of those women? Did he have a girlfriend?"

"Not that I know of. Those girls were strangers around here. He'd hook up with girls he met at The

Tavern sometimes. That's the thing. He liked that girl, Brandy. Why would he want to kill her?"

The story going around must be that Tony killed all the women, including Brandy. Chuck would be relieved to find out later that at least Tony wasn't responsible for Brandy's death, but Grayson wasn't the one to tell him.

"Was Brandy his girlfriend?" Grayson rubbed his palms on the thighs of his jeans.

"Nah, just friends, I think. What do the kids call it these days? Friends with benefits? Something like that." Chuck nodded toward Zane at the end of the dock, clipboard in hand. "If you ask me, there's trouble right there."

"Zane? What do you mean? Do you think he had anything to do with the murders?"

"If he did, the cops would've arrested him, too. But Zane was into drugs and hung out with a shady crowd. Tony started running with the same bunch once he met Zane here at work. Maybe it was my fault for getting Tony a job on the docks."

Grayson smacked Chuck on the back. "Don't blame yourself for anything. If it did go down like they're saying, Tony's the only one to blame."

About an hour later, after Chuck left early to support his sister, Grayson wandered over to Zane, who was clutching his clipboard with one hand and his phone with the other.

Grayson tipped up his chin. "Did you record that last pallet? Chuck left early, but Bruce stepped in."

"Got it." Zane drummed his pencil on his clipboard in a staccato beat.

"Hey—" Grayson glanced over his shoulder "—did you know what Tony was doing in his spare time?"

Zane dropped his pencil and stooped to pick it up, his face reddening to the roots of his hair. "Hell, no. Why does everyone keep asking me that? We were buds and hung out. I never knew he was a serial killer."

"Serial killer?" Grayson cocked his head. "I never heard that. I thought it was some drug thing. You know, the girls were working for him and stole some money. Something like that."

"Tony?" Zane's eyes rounded and bulged from their sockets. "You think Tony was running the show?"

Grayson spread his hands. "Someone's gotta run the show, right? You know, in my day, before weed was legal in Michigan, we always kind of knew who was in charge."

"It sure as hell wasn't Tony." Zane narrowed his eyes. "You have any weed on you now?"

"On the job? Are you kidding? Anyway, I thought maybe Tony was second-in-command." Grayson got close enough to Zane to see the red veins in his eyes. "Even I know the top dog around these parts for dance fever is V…or should I say the top bitch?"

Zane dug his uneven teeth into his bottom lip. "Damn, you know about V?"

"I think it's common knowledge if you hang with the right people. Do you hang with the right people, Zane?"

He puffed out his scrawny chest. "I know everyone."

"I thought you did." The adrenaline was racing through Grayson's body and he clenched his hands in his pockets. "I heard V's got it goin' on, too. Heard she's a dime piece."

Zane wrinkled his nose. "Yeah, she might be okay for old dudes like you, but her sister? She's a smoke show."

"Her sister?" Grayson's heart thudded in his chest. "She's in town?"

"Just moved here. You probably seen her at The Tavern. Rita. Rita Beaulieu."

MAX SLIPPED HEAVILY into a chair at the conference table and chugged down half a can of soda. He dragged a tissue across his nose and balled it in his fist. "Carly and I hit up every informant known to PHPD—at least, those we could reach. The good news is we have a first name for V. The bad news is it's a pretty common first name—Victoria."

Carly shrugged off her coat where it pooled around her in the chair. "We hit up PHPD vice, and they combed through their files. No Victoria, very few women drug dealers at all, and none currently operating in this area."

Aria tapped a pen against her chin. "Victoria is even a name Tony came up with when he was brainstorming, but I don't think it had any significance to him."

"It's something." Alana folded her hands on the table. "More than one informant gave you the name?"

Max held up two fingers. "Two, and while a few more claimed not to know her name, they did verify that a dealer known as V was working the area. So, we did get some confirmation. Our boy Tony came through."

Axel pointed at Aria. "Furry slippers on order."

"Then we concentrate on finding Victoria. Before we get out of here and break for some dinner, Selena and Blanca found a similar pattern at the other murder sights. Selena?" Alana nodded at the K-9 handler.

Selena coughed. "Opaline, do you have those photos I sent you ready?"

"Of course, I *do* know my job." The TV screen on the wall came to life, displaying the same type of gravel walkway next to the lake where Chloe's body had been found.

"This is Jane Doe number one's murder site." Selena aimed a red laser pointer at the screen and circled an area in the reeds by the water. "Blanca alerted next to the lake, as she did at Chloe Larsen's crime scene. And the same for Jane Doe number three's... Opaline?"

"On it." Opaline brushed cracker crumbs from the table into her palm and brought up the next slide.

Aria's gaze darted between the two sisters. She'd hate to spend Christmas with the Lopez family.

Her phone buzzed on the table in front of her and she swept it off. Resting it in her lap, she glanced at Grayson's text. Her gasp nearly choked her and drew all eyes in the room.

Alana raised her eyebrows. "Something you need to share with us, Aria?"

She lifted her head and met Alana's eyes. "I know Victoria's real name...and where we can find her."

Chapter Eighteen

On Grayson's information, Max and Carly headed down to PHPD vice to run the name "Victoria Beaulieu" past them, and Opaline got to work on several databases to check for both Victoria and Rita Beaulieu.

"Amanda, order some pizza for us. It's going to be a long night." Alana took a seat across from Aria and Axel. "If I'd known how valuable having someone at the docks would've been, we could've put one of our own in there. But picking up on his sister's reference to the docks, Mr. Rhodes has worked out quite nicely."

"He has." Aria picked up a bottle and gulped back some water. Why did her cheeks have to heat up like a sixteen-year-old girl's every time someone on the team mentioned Grayson?

"Uh—" Axel picked up the half-empty bottle of water and shook it "—this was my water."

"Oops, sorry. I'm not sick or anything, I promise." Aria made a cross over her heart.

"Axel, I'd like you and Aria to track down Rita Beaulieu while Carly and Max continue working with the informants to get to her sister, Victoria." Alana called over her shoulder to Opaline, "You have an address on Rita yet?"

"Coming up. I'll be sending it to Axel's and Aria's phones." Opaline's long nails clicked on the keyboard. "Nothing on Victoria, but that's to be expected. Rita hasn't been associated with this address for very long, so maybe it's actually her sister's. We can hope."

Aria tapped her phone to receive the address Opaline had sent, an address not far from Grayson's motel. "What I don't get is that Rita is the one who carried a note to Grayson for Brandy. Why would she jeopardize her sister's smuggling ring?"

"You're assuming Rita knows what her sister does for a living. She may have been completely in the dark." Axel held up his phone to Opaline. "Got it, thanks. Let's enlighten Rita."

Axel drove to Rita's last-known address in a sketchy area of Port Huron. He tapped on his window, toward the building. "You'd think her sister would've warned Rita what areas to avoid in town."

"Unless Victoria lives with her and can protect her. It makes a good cover for V."

"Don't get your hopes up. Even if she does live with her sister, V may know we're onto her. I hardly think she'll be reclining on the sofa, watching TV, waiting for our arrival." He pulled up across the street from an apartment building with a set of stairs on the outside and an overflowing Dumpster, not quite hidden at the side of the building.

Aria released her seat belt. "Not quite what I expected from a drug lord."

As they jogged across the street, Axel said, "Number four."

They reached the base of the stairs and Aria ducked her head beneath it. "The odds are downstairs—one and three down here, so two and four must be upstairs."

"I'll go first. Stay behind me. Don't draw your weapon, but be ready."

Aria followed Axel up the stairs, her hand hovering over her gun tucked into the holster on her hip, beneath her jacket. A low light burned inside number four, and Axel stood to the side and rapped on the door with his knuckle.

No noise or voice responded.

Axel knocked again, this time calling out, "Rita? Rita, are you there?"

The door to number two cracked open and Aria stepped back to get a clear view, her hand resting on the butt of her mm.

A man poked his head through the space. "You looking for Rita?"

Axel stepped away from Rita's door. "Is she home? Do you know where she is?"

"Gone. Who are you?"

Aria stepped in front of his door. "Gone, gone? Or gone, out for the evening?"

"She's gone, gone. Who are you?"

Axel flicked open his badge. "FBI. We have a few questions for Rita. She's not in trouble or anything."

"Yeah, that's what you think." The man shook his gray head.

"Sir, can you please step outside? Show yourself?" Aria held out her own badge to the crack of the door.

The crack widened to reveal an old man with faded blue eyes and gray scruff on his chin that could pass for a beard in a certain light—not this one.

"My name's Hal Bernard. What do you wanna question Rita about?"

"Mr. Bernard, what did you mean when you said Rita was in trouble?"

"She came back here last night in a big hurry, tires squealing and everything. Ran right upstairs, and I heard a bunch of banging around, so I knocked on her door to see what was going on, and she was packing up. Said she had to leave 'toot sweet.'" Hal winked. "That's 'very fast' in French."

"Thanks for the translation." Aria was close enough to Hal to smell the booze on his breath, but then she could also be downstairs for that. "Did she say why she was leaving?"

"People come." Hal shrugged his narrow, sloped shoulders. "People go."

"What makes you think she left because she was in trouble?" Axel folded his arms and took a deep breath that expanded his chest, making himself look larger than he was. Her brothers always pulled the same trick on her.

It worked on Hal, as he seemed to snap to attention. "It was what happened after."

Aria asked, "Happened after she packed up?"

"That's right. She dragged her bags down the stairs—" Hal lifted his chin "—I helped her. After she loaded her car, another car came tearing up. The woman that got out of the car tried to talk to Rita, but Rita wasn't having any. She screamed and yelled at the woman…had flashbacks to my ex-wife."

Axel shot her a look from the corner of his eye. "What were they arguing about?"

"I dunno, tried to tune it out and get the hell away from them." He bunched his shoulders and faked a shiver in memory.

"You didn't hear anything they said, even though Rita was yelling?" Aria tapped the toe of her boot.

"Something about a warehouse. Rita was screaming that she saw the warehouse, and I don't know." Hal scratched his grizzled whiskers. "Maybe there was booze in the warehouse."

"Booze?" Axel braced a hand on the stucco wall. "What makes you say that?"

"Because Rita was screaming something about brandy—that's it. Brandy, warehouse, and that she was leaving town. Don't call her. Don't find her."

Aria's pulse jumped in her throat. "Did you hear the other woman's name?"

"No, but I seen her before."

Axel asked, "Where?"

"Right here. She visited Rita before—and they might be related."

"Why do you think that?" Aria ran her tongue along her bottom lip.

"They both had that black hair, both lookers." Hal nudged Axel. "If you know what I mean."

"I know exactly what you mean, Hal."

They tried to get more information out of Hal about the other woman's car, what she looked like, specifically, her other visits to Rita, but Hal had reached his limit—and his limit was pretty good.

They both handed Hal their cards and walked back to the car—in Aria's case, more like bounced. When Axel got behind the wheel, she turned to him and grabbed his arm. "That was V. Rita must've discovered her sister's side gig and freaked out, knowing Victoria was responsible for Brandy's murder."

"And there's a warehouse." Axel pulled out his phone. "That's clearly where and how Rita found out about her sister."

Aria listened, her legs bouncing up and down as Axel got on the phone to Alana, putting her on Speaker.

He described their meeting with Hal. "We need info on a warehouse, Alana. Get Opaline on it right now. Maybe she rented it in Rita's name. My guess is it's by the docks. V needs to be close to the water."

"Don't come back in, yet. You're on speaker phone, and Opaline has already started searching Port Huron for warehouses near the water. Max and Carly didn't get any hits on Victoria Beaulieu from PHPD vice. She's not on their radar."

Aria said to Axel, "While we're waiting, I'm going to see if the manager can let me into Rita's apartment. I saw a manager sign on number one. Maybe she left something behind."

"Do you want me to go with you?"

"No, I'm good. You wait on the phone with Alana. I'm just going to take a quick look around." Aria reached into the back seat and grabbed an FBI jacket. She slid from the passenger seat and stuffed her arms into the windbreaker, pulling it over her leather jacket. Ducking her head into the car, she said, "Just in case he needs some convincing."

"You look convincing to me. Go get 'em."

Aria crossed the street again and knocked on apartment number one, the gold Manager sign nailed to the wall next to the door.

A woman's smoke-roughened voice came from the other side of the door. "Who is it?"

"FBI, ma'am. I'm wondering if I can have a look in Rita Beaulieu's apartment, number four upstairs?" Aria flipped out her badge and held it up to the peephole.

The manager swung open the door and straightened her red wig. "You don't have to tell me which apartment it is. That girl hightailed it out of here, breaking her lease."

"Did you hear the argument she had with the woman in the parking lot before she left, Mrs...?"

"Hammond." She cracked her gum on the left side of her mouth. "Got a blow-by-blow from Hal upstairs. She do something wrong, that girl? Besides run out on her lease?"

"We just wanted to talk to her, but it might be helpful if I can have a look around her place. Did she leave anything behind?"

"A few odds and ends." Mrs. Hammond was already pulling a set of keys from her pocket. She plucked one from the ring, the rest dangling from her fingers in front of Aria. "Here's the master. You're welcome to look around and then drop these in my box when you're done."

"Thank you, Mrs. Hammond." As Aria clomped up the stairs, she glanced at Axel still in the car across the street. She passed Hal's apartment, wondering if he had his eye to the peephole or his ear to the wall.

She let herself into the apartment, the light from a lamp in the corner casting shadows in the corners. The place must've come furnished because a sofa, one chair, a table and a small dinette set remained.

Aria started with the bedroom, but Rita had emptied the closet and drawers. Even the sheets had been ripped off the queen bed.

She returned to the living room, but Rita had cleared out this room, as well. Four long steps took Aria right into the small kitchen and she opened the fridge. A few beer bottles rattled and a couple of condiments fell over in the door. Rita was not much of a cook.

Aria pulled open some drawers and thumbed through some paper receipts and take-out menus. Some circular cardboard coasters fanned out in the drawer, and Aria began collecting and stacking them.

She jumped when the front door burst open.

Axel called into the room. "It's go time. We have a warehouse listed under Rita's name."

Aria shoved the coasters into the pocket of her leather jacket and exited the apartment, locking the door behind her. When they reached the foot of the stairs, she veered toward Mrs. Hammond's door and dropped the keys in the box.

When they got to the car, Axel took off before she even closed the door. "Is it near the docks?"

"Not too far from where Max found one of those tunnels." Axel took the next turn at high speed and Aria gripped the edge of the seat.

They made it from Rita's apartment to the docks in just under fifteen minutes and were the first ones on the scene. Axel squealed to a stop. As he got out of the car, he pointed to a row of gray warehouses away from the loading zone and on the other side of the water from the marina with the pleasure boats.

Axel took off running, his long legs putting him far ahead of Aria. He disappeared around the corner of a building. As she scrambled to keep up with him, gunshots echoed over the water. She pulled her gun from its holster, her legs pumping, her feet pounding against the asphalt almost as much as her heart.

She reached the building and skidded to a stop. With her gun raised to her chest, gripped in both hands, she yelled, "Axel!"

"I'm okay. Stay down. They got away, but they have to be in the area."

Panting, Aria crouched and poked her head around the corner of the building. Her heart stuttered for a second as she spotted Axel flat on the ground. "You all right?"

"They didn't hit me, and I don't think I hit them. The two of them took off out of that warehouse at the end."

Engines roared and tires squealed behind Aria. She cranked her head over her shoulder. "The cavalry's here. If you wanna give chase, I got you covered."

Axel rose to his haunches and Aria's muscles twitched with tension as he propelled himself forward and behind a wall. No more shots rang out.

When the other agents crowded behind her, Aria gave a quick account of the situation. "Axel saw two people leave the warehouse at the end. One of them exchanged fire with Axel. Nobody hit. They took off in the other direction."

Alana ordered Max, Carly and Selena, Blanca primed and ready at her side, to fan out around the back side of the warehouses. "Go through the loading docks if you have to. We didn't see any cars pull away. They have to still be on foot."

Axel continued his approach toward the warehouse, jumping from cover to cover, and Aria kept after him. When he reached the warehouse, he yanked up the overhead door, which had been left ajar.

Aria joined him as the door rolled up, both agents with their guns pointed in front of them. The squeaking ended and Aria took a breath as her gaze darted around the mostly empty warehouse. "Looks like Rita's place. Someone left in a hurry."

"And with guns blazing." Axel's blue eyes had their own fire. "It was her, Aria. I had V in my sights, and she got away."

Chapter Nineteen

The disappointment socked Aria in the gut. To be so close and have her slip through their fingers. If they'd come here before Rita's place, they would've caught V in the act. But they wouldn't have known about the warehouse without going to Rita's and talking to chatty Hal.

Aria blew out a breath. "Maybe she won't get away. The others are here, and they're hot on her tail."

Alana strode toward them, her gun primed and ready. "Nothing?"

"I wouldn't say 'nothing.'" Aria stepped into the warehouse, her boots ringing on the cement floor. "They didn't have time to clear out everything."

"Was it V, Axel?" Alana asked.

"A tall woman with black hair. She had a gun, but it was her henchman doing the shooting. They just seemed to disappear into thin air." Axel shook his head.

Max circled around from the other side and lifted his arms, shrugging. "Poof. Gone."

"I saw nothing, but I heard the engine of a boat."

Carly jogged up to them and ducked into the warehouse. "But what do we have here? Looks like packaging."

"V probably made a last stop here to collect whatever she has left to start somewhere fresh." Axel banged against the wall of the warehouse with his fist.

Selena was the last to join them, Blanca trotting by her side. "Water. They left by water. Blanca tracked them to a small jetty where they could've easily had a boat waiting."

"That's it. She's gone." Axel holstered his gun, which he'd been holding as if expecting V to saunter back into his sight.

"I'm counting on those tunnels. If V still has product in this area, she's not going anywhere without it. She may be the big fish around Port Huron and Point Edward, but she answers to a bigger fish—and that shark is not going to allow product to be left behind." Alana clapped her hands. "I know it's late, people, and you're tired and disappointed, but we have a warehouse to search."

THE FOLLOWING NIGHT, Aria sat with her team after dinner, discussing their next move with V. Alana was convinced their prey was still in the Port Huron area, taking care of last-minute business, but they had a small window.

"Not that we can't follow V to her next location." Alana dropped her napkin on the table. "She doesn't know us if she thinks we're going to give up that easily."

"Hi, all. Sorry I missed dinner." Rihanna strutted across the dining-room floor looking like a model on a runway. "But you all dumped a lot of work in my lap with that raid on the warehouse last night, and I have another dinner to go to in a less than an hour."

"News is out there, but nobody knows V, huh?" Carly stretched her long arms over her head, catlike, and yawned.

Opaline answered. "We don't have her official picture, but we do have a sketch artist working on a composite. If she's lurking around Port Huron, she'll be spotted."

"Although V does seem to be partial to hair dye, like someone I know." Selena flicked her fingers at her sister's lavender locks. "She could dye that black hair blond or brown, cut it, change her makeup. She could completely disguise herself."

Axel pushed away his plate. "Or just send her minions out to collect what's left in the tunnels and tie up any loose ends."

"Ugh, so morose." Rihanna snatched a fry from Max's plate. "I do have good news, though."

Rihanna held up the French fry, waiting for all eyes on her. Then she turned her gaze toward Aria. "The DNA results came in, and Grayson Rhodes and little Danny are definitely related. He can take custody of his nephew as early as tomorrow."

A smile tugged at Aria's lips even as pain tugged at her heart, knowing this meant Grayson would be returning to Detroit. He'd probably forget that he'd even asked her to help vet his nanny.

"That is great news, Rihanna. Does he know?" Aria's hand felt for her phone in her pocket. Grayson hadn't texted her at all today—not that she hadn't been busy processing evidence from the warehouse.

"I called him when I received the news, right before I got here." Rihanna picked up her phone in its jeweled case and glanced at the display. "Which means he should be calling you in five, four, three…"

Aria laughed along with the others. What did she have to lose now? The case in Port Huron was probably finished. Grayson would be taking Danny back to Detroit. Aria had already lost everything.

Team members began to wander away from the table. Max had a video date with his son over the phone. Opaline had an actual date with Gordon the PHPD cop. Axel and Selena were heading off to spend some time with Blanca. Carly planned to go for a run and Rihanna had a dinner meeting. Alana and Amanda were going to spend another hour in Alana's room to finish some reports.

Feeling as low as the others looked, Aria shuffled back to her room and fell across her bed. A minute later, her cell phone rang. The name on the display made her heart flutter—still.

"Grayson, I heard the good news."

"That's right. I can pick up Danny from the Colbys tomorrow. My mother actually got back to me, and was heartbroken over Chloe, despite everything. She's promised to visit her grandson the next time she sets foot on American soil."

"That's good to hear." Aria curled up into a ball. "Does this mean you're leaving your job? Port Huron?"

"I've already told the supervisor, Bud. He's going

to make up a story for the other guys, but yeah, today was my last day."

"Again, we can't thank you enough for the part you played in solving this case. Your presence at the docks was invaluable to us and a great personal risk to you."

"That all sounds so formal. I called because I want to see you before I leave. You haven't forgotten your promise, have you?"

Aria closed her eyes and swallowed the lump in her throat. "I haven't forgotten. Do you want to come here this time?"

If he thought his own motel was too crummy for making love, would this one work?

"Actually, I'd like to meet at the marina. It's a cold night, but clear. Maybe we can have a piece of pie at that diner where we first met."

Aria bounded from the bed. "I'd love that. Forty-five minutes?"

Grayson agreed, and Aria ended the call and darted around the hotel room to get ready. She shimmied out of her grungy jeans and slipped into a pair of skinny black jeans. She pulled on a soft, coral sweater, a pair of black boots with a heel and grabbed her leather jacket.

She met Carly in the hallway, coming back from her run. Carly paused at her door. "Are you okay?"

"Couldn't be better. I'm heading to the marina to see Grayson." Aria waved a hand in the air as she got into the elevator.

She drove more carefully than she ever had before. It wouldn't do to get into an accident on her way to what might be her last time seeing Grayson.

As she pulled into the parking lot of the diner, Grayson waved from where he stood, leaning against his beat-up truck. He'd already told her he planned to give that truck to Will when he left.

When she reached him, he pulled her into his arms, wrapping them snugly around her, and kissed her. He murmured against her mouth, "I missed you. Do you really think I can return to Detroit without you?"

"How is that going to work, Grayson?" She placed her hands against his chest, and his heart thundered beneath her palm. She curled her fingers around the collar of his flannel shirt. "I want to be with you, but I have this job."

"Let's walk." He draped his arm around her shoulders, and led her toward the boats in all their multicolored splendor.

She rested her head against his upper arm. "I like the tradition of decorating boats for Christmas. They're beautiful, aren't they?"

"You're beautiful." He stroked her hair. "We can figure this out, Aria. I can pretty much run my business from home. I'll be there with Danny and the nanny you're going to help me select."

The clanking halyards almost sounded like church bells pealing. Maybe it was some kind of sign.

She sighed and shoved her hands into her pockets. Her fingers traced the rounded edge of hard cardboard, and she pulled it out. She held it in front of her and squinted in the dark.

"What's that?" Grayson flicked the edge of the cardboard with his finger.

"Oh, yeah. I picked them up in Rita's apartment. They're coasters from a restaurant or something." She turned on her phone's flashlight and illuminated a coaster, turning it over in her hand.

"Beautiful Place?" Grayson's brow furrowed. "That sounds familiar."

"It does, doesn't it? A restaurant near your motel?"

"A beautiful place near *my* motel? I don't think so." He snapped his fingers. "I remember. It's the name of a boat down here. We walked past it on our way to *Fun Times* to meet Brandy. What do you think Rita was doing with coasters from a big boat like that? Party?"

Aria dropped the coaster and grabbed Grayson's arm. "Beautiful place… Beaulieu."

"Huh? You lost me. What does beautiful place have to do with Victoria Beaulieu?"

Her fingers dug into the arm of his jacket. "*Beaulieu* means beautiful place. That's V's boat. I know it. That's how she's been able to come and go at that warehouse. That's how she's been able to stay below the radar in Port Huron. She's on that boat."

The adrenaline pumped through Aria's system and she spun around on the marina, the Christmas lights blurring in her vision. "Where was it? Where were those slips?"

The FBI had already towed away *Fun Times* for additional processing, and Aria's excitement was adding to her confusion.

"*Fun Times* was in slip 128. *Beautiful Place* is in the same row." Grayson seemed to have better bearings than she did at this moment, and he grabbed her hand and tugged her in the other direction. "It's one over."

Aria's hands trembled as she tapped her phone for Alana's number. "I'm calling the team, but we can't wait. We missed V once already at the warehouse. We can't afford to miss her again, or she'll be gone."

Amanda answered and Aria spit out directions, sounding incoherent to herself, but Amanda must've understood.

Aria cursed her heels as she and Grayson ran across the marina and turned toward the slip that housed *Beautiful Place*. In the still night, an engine rumbled to life.

Grayson cursed. "It must be her. She has someone looking out. The minute anyone comes her way, the boat sets out on the lake."

"They're gonna have company this time." She scanned the other boats in the slips. "Do you know how to drive a boat?"

"You're kidding, right?" He swept past her and jumped onto the first boat in line. "And I know where most boaters hide their keys."

Twisting her fingers in front of her, Aria called out, "Hurry, they're getting away."

Grayson jumped into the next boat with no better luck. The third boat he dismissed as too small. From inside the fourth boat, he shouted, "Got 'em."

Aria climbed into the boat just has Grayson started the engine. She clung to the edge. "Can you cut the lights?"

"Not if you don't want to crash into something in the marina. They'll have to know we're coming after them, but V's boat is made for comfort. This baby—" he patted the steering wheel "—she's made for speed."

To emphasize his point, Grayson revved the engine and then zipped out of the marina onto the lake. He pointed. "I see them."

"Do they see us?"

"If not, they soon will." Grayson pushed the stolen powerboat to its limits as he followed in the bigger boat's wake. The choppy, frigid water sprayed into the boat, hitting Aria's face, but she never took her eyes off the *Beautiful Place*.

V's boat sped up, but was no match for the power beneath her and Grayson. As they drew closer to the big boat, the lights went out, sending a chill through Aria's body.

They tagged along behind *Beautiful Place* and then Grayson made a move to pull up beside it. That's when the bullets started flying.

"They're shooting. Get down."

Aria crouched, her gun leveled at the deck of *Beautiful Place*. When a bullet pinged off their boat's fiberglass, Aria squeezed off several shots. She didn't know how much longer they'd be able to hold off V, but hoped it was long enough for the rest of the team or the Coast Guard to get out here.

Grayson gunned the boat and yelled. "Stay down and hold on, Aria. I'm gonna try something crazy."

She sank to the deck, clutching the edge. Grayson fired a few times from his own gun, which she didn't even realize he had with him.

When the explosion hit, it lifted their boat off the

lake and a fireball rolled across the water in front of them. Intense heat scorched the air, and Aria held her breath.

Grayson cut the engine and swung the boat around toward the *Beautiful Place*, now engulfed by flames, black smoke belching from the masts that looked like matchsticks ready to topple over.

A woman screamed, and Aria hung over the side of the boat, dragging a lifesaver to the edge.

V and a man paddled frantically away from the inferno, both clinging to debris from the wreckage.

Grayson jumped down beside Aria and waved ash away from her face. "Are you all right? I hit the gas tank. I figured that was the best way to stop them."

Aria clambered to her knees, aiming her gun over the side of the boat, V in her bull's-eye. "Of course, I'm fine. Haven't I told you? I'm a special agent for the FBI."

Epilogue

Amanda studied the décor, her head tilted, her red hair sweeping over one shoulder. "Is it too much? Tell me the truth."

Aria blinked at all the Christmas lights, the little individual Christmas trees at every table and the Santa in the corner, keeping up a steady stream of ho, ho, ho's.

"It's pretty, but maybe the Santa..."

"The Santa is hideous and annoying." Opaline crowded in next to them, a plate of crab rolls, won tons and mini *taquitos* balanced on one hand. "Get rid of him."

Amanda laughed. "I knew I could depend on you for the truth, Opaline."

Max walked up and put his hand on Amanda's shoulder. "I'm going to the bar. Drink orders?"

"I'm going to get rid of Santa first before he drives everyone crazy." Amanda scurried away.

"White wine for me, please." Opaline examined a crab roll. "Do you think these have a lot of calories, Aria?"

"If it's fried, it has a lot of calories." Carly held up a stick of celery.

Opaline turned up her nose. "I wasn't asking you, Carly. Aria?"

"Yeah, I'm afraid Carly's right." Aria tapped her chest. "I'll have a white wine, too."

"Oh, are you taking drink orders?" Carly raised her eyebrows at Max. "You owe me after dragging me around the underbelly of Port Huron for three hours talking to lowlifes."

Max crooked his finger at Carly. "You're coming with me because I'm pretty sure I'm not gonna get your drink order right."

"Good call." Carly followed Max to the bartender set up in the corner.

Selena held out a plate to Aria. "Take something. The *taquitos* are good. Gringo food, but good."

Aria picked up the appetizer and blew on it. "This is nice. Do you always have a party at the end of a case, or is this for Christmas?"

"It's both—definitely doubling as our Christmas bash and a celebration of the closing of the case, thanks to you." Selena waved as Axel entered the room. He pointed to the bottle of beer in his hand and Selena nodded.

"And thanks to Blanca for finally discovering those tunnels." Aria crunched into the *taquito*.

"With a little help from V—once she recovered from her burns and near drowning."

Alana and Rihanna finally finished their conversation at one of the tables and walked over to the group, drinks in hand.

Rihanna spun around in place. "Amanda outdid herself this time. I'm ready to break into a Christmas carol—and I'm glad she got rid of that Santa."

"Someone had to tell her." Opaline pushed back her green-tinted ends.

Rihanna flicked Opaline's hair. "You disappoint, Opaline. I would've expected green on one side and red on the other for Christmas."

Max returned, carrying a beer and one glass of wine, which he handed to Aria. Carly followed him with Opaline's wine and a martini glass with an onion and an olive hanging off the side.

Axel joined them with beers for him and Selena. "With this setup, you must've invited more than just us."

"Some members of the PHPD are joining us—the guys from the dive team, some members of Vice. Detective Massey is coming, and a few others."

"Gordon." Opaline held up her wineglass and Alana tapped it with hers.

"Gordon, of course." Alana asked Axel, "Is Tony Balducci all settled in his new home?"

"He is, but I think he's safe from V for now. She wasn't high enough in the organization to warrant any retaliation on her behalf. The cartel has dismissed her. She's the one who'd better watch her back in prison."

Selena put down her plate of food and wiped her hands. "Did V ever confirm that the murdered blah boaties were stealing from her?"

"She claimed they were, but she was paranoid." Axel

tipped some beer down his throat. "We may never know the truth, but she felt she had to get rid of those women and she wanted to set them up as being involved in the drug trade, never imagining it would lead straight back to her."

The noise level of the room increased as some of the invited guests began arriving for the party. Before they lost this moment, before they got back to their normal professional roles, Aria touched Alana's shoulder. "How are you doing?"

Alana smiled, a little mistily. "I'm fine. It was a tough case for me. I'm not going to lie, but I appreciate your listening to me and your discretion."

"Of course. Always."

Rihanna squealed from across the room. "It's our boy!"

Aria jerked her head toward the door and a warm feeling encased her heart as she saw Grayson holding Danny.

Rihanna held out her arms and Grayson poured Danny into them.

Cuddling the baby against her chest, Rihanna danced across the room. "Look who I have. My favorite little man."

Carly dipped her head toward Aria's. "And yours—only Grayson isn't so little."

Aria opened her mouth to protest and then snapped it shut as her gaze traveled from Carly's face to Selena's to Opaline's, and rested on Alana's.

Selena snorted. "You don't think it was a secret,

do you? The fact that you were falling for Grayson Rhodes?"

"I… I just thought. I mean…"

Alana squeezed her hand. "Go to him, Aria. It's all right."

With her eyes stinging, Aria crossed the room slowly, all the noise, the people, the music, the singing, even Santa now silent and stuffed in the corner, fading from her senses. She only saw the man in front of her.

As she drew closer, he reached out for her and pulled her outside the banquet room, away from the party. He led her to a dark corner by the window where the lights of the boats in the marina blinked.

They sat on a red-velvet love seat, her hands still in his. "H-how is Danny?"

"He's going to be fine. I have that list of nannies whenever you're ready."

She pulled his hands against her chest. "Can we really do this? Does it make sense?"

"I love you, Aria. I know I never want to be without you by my side—and I don't mean that literally. If we're together, in each other's corners, in each other's hearts, it'll all make sense in the end."

"I…" She closed her eyes and Grayson touched her cheek.

"Go ahead. Tell me your concerns. Tell me your worries. Tell me why we can't be together. You may be the FBI agent, but I'll shoot them all down."

"Concerns? Worries?" She brought his hands to her lips and kissed his knuckles, rough from his work on the docks. "I was just going to say I love you, too."

He slipped his hand behind her head and pressed his mouth against hers in a scorching kiss that incinerated all her doubts and promised everything.

* * * * *

#1965 TOXIN ALERT
Tactical Crime Division: Traverse City • by Tyler Anne Snell
After a deadly anthrax attack on Amish land, TCD's biological weapons expert Carly Welsh must work with rancher Noah Miller to get information from the distrustful members of the community. But even their combined courage and smarts might not be enough against the sinister forces at work.

#1966 TEXAS LAW
An O'Connor Family Mystery • by Barb Han
Sheriff Colton O'Connor never expected to see Makena Eden again. But after she darts in front of his car one night, the spark that was lit between Makena and Colton long ago reignites. With a rogue cop tracking them, will they walk away—together?

#1967 COWBOY UNDER FIRE
The Justice Seekers • by Lena Diaz
Following the death of her friend, Hayley Nash turns to former cop Dalton Lynch for help. Dalton finds working with the web expert to be an exercise in restraint—especially when it comes to keeping his hands to himself.

#1968 MOUNTAIN OF EVIDENCE
The Ranger Brigade: Rocky Mountain Manhunt
by Cindi Myers
Eve Shea's ex is missing. Although her romantic feelings for the man are long gone, her honor demands she be a part of Ranger Commander Grant Sanderlin's investigation. But as more clues emerge, is Eve's ex a victim—or a killer targeting the woman Grant is falling for?

#1969 CRIME SCENE COVER-UP
The Taylor Clan: Firehouse 13 • by Julie Miller
Mark Taylor can put out a fire, but Amy Hall is a different kind of challenge. He's determined to keep her safe—but she's just as certain that she doesn't need his protection. As they hunt down an arsonist, will they trust each other enough to surrender...before a madman burns down their world?

#1970 THE LAST RESORT
by Janice Kay Johnson
When Leah Keaton arrives at her family's mountain resort, armed insurgents capture her, but Spencer Wyatt, the group's second in command, takes her under his protection. Spencer is an undercover FBI agent, but to keep Leah safe, he's willing to risk his mission—and his life.

SPECIAL EXCERPT FROM

⟨H⟩HARLEQUIN

INTRIGUE

*Sheriff Colton O'Connor is stunned when a stormy night
brings him face-to-face with a woman from his past.
Seeing Makena Eden again is a shock to his system...
especially once he realizes she's hiding something. As
the rain turns torrential, Colton has to get to the heart
of what Makena is doing in his small hometown. And
why her once-vibrant eyes look so incredibly haunted...*

Keep reading for a sneak peek at
Texas Law, *part of An O'Connor Family Mystery,
from* USA TODAY *bestselling author Barb Han.*

Makena needed medical attention. That part was obvious. The
tricky part was going to be getting her looked at. He was still
trying to wrap his mind around the fact Makena Eden was
sitting in his SUV.

Talk about a blast from the past and a missed opportunity.
But he couldn't think about that right now when she was injured.
At least she was eating. That had to be a good sign.

When she'd tried to stand, she'd gone down pretty fast and
hard. She'd winced in pain and he'd scooped her up and brought
her to his vehicle. He knew better than to move an injured
person. In this case, however, there was no choice.

The victim was alert and cognizant of what was going on.
A quick visual scan of her body revealed nothing obviously
broken. No bones were sticking out. She complained about her
hip and he figured there could be something there. At the very
least, she needed an X-ray.

Since getting to the county hospital looked impossible at least in the short run and his apartment was close by, he decided taking her to his place might be for the best until the roads cleared. He could get her out of his uncomfortable vehicle and onto a soft couch.

Normally, he wouldn't take a stranger to his home, but this was Makena. And even though he hadn't seen her in forever, she'd been special to him at one time.

He still needed to check on the RV for Mrs. Dillon…and then it dawned on him. Was Makena the "tenant" the widow had been talking about earlier?

"Are you staying in town?" he asked, hoping to get her to volunteer the information. It was possible that she'd fallen on hard times and needed a place to hang her head for a couple of nights.

"I've been staying in a friend's RV," she said. So, she was the "tenant" Mrs. Dillon had mentioned.

It was good seeing Makena again. At five feet five inches, she had a body made for sinning underneath a thick head of black hair. He remembered how shiny and wavy her hair used to be. Even soaked with water, it didn't look much different now.

She had the most honest set of pale blue eyes—eyes the color of the sky on an early summer morning. She had the kind of eyes that he could stare into all day. It had been like that before, too.

But that was a long time ago. And despite the lightning bolt that had struck him square in the chest when she turned to face him, this relationship was purely professional.

Don't miss
Texas Law *by Barb Han,*
available December 2020 wherever
Harlequin Intrigue books and ebooks are sold.

Harlequin.com